A WISH FOR WINGS

Also available by Robert Swindells,
and published by Doubleday/Corgi Yearling Books:

ABOMINATION
HYDRA
INSIDE THE WORM
INVISIBLE!
JACQUELINE HYDE
NIGHTMARE STAIRS
ROOM 13
TIMESNATCH
THE THOUSAND EYES OF NIGHT

STONECOLD year 8.

non-fiction Year 9.
Newspapers

A WISH
FOR WINGS

ROBERT SWINDELLS

DOUBLEDAY

LONDON · NEW YORK · TORONTO · SYDNEY · AUCKLAND

TRANSWORLD PUBLISHERS
61–63 Uxbridge Road, London W5 5SA
A division of The Random House Group Ltd.

RANDOM HOUSE AUSTRALIA (PTY) LTD
20 Alfred Street, Milsons Point, Sydney,
New South Wales 2061, Australia

RANDOM HOUSE NEW ZEALAND LTD
18 Poland Road, Glenfield, Auckland 10, New Zealand

RANDOM HOUSE (PTY) LTD
Endulini, 5A Jubilee Road, Parktown 2193, South Africa

Published 2001 by Doubleday
a division of Transworld Publishers

A catalogue record for this book is available
from the British Library

ISBN 0 385 410417

2 4 6 8 10 9 7 5 3

Set in 12/15.5pt Century Old Style by
Falcon Oast Graphic Art

Printed in Great Britain
by
Mackays of Chatham plc,
Chatham, Kent

For My Grandchildren
Catherine, Christopher and Nikki
Who made an old man proud and happy

'. . . Such a strong wish for wings, –
wings such as wealth can furnish . . .'

from a letter written by Charlotte Brontë
to Ellen Nussey, 7th August 1841

A WISH FOR WINGS

One

'I'm going to be an airline captain,' announced Jenna one teatime when she was nearly fourteen.

'Are you, dear?' said her mother dreamily, gazing out the window. 'Looks like rain again.'

'Hmmm,' mumbled Dad, spooning raspberry jam onto his scone, 'that'll make a change.'

The only person who actually *heard* Jenna's announcement was her fifteen-year-old brother Ned, and he put her down as usual. 'Airline captain,' he scoffed. 'Have you ever *seen* a woman airline captain, Sis?' He didn't give her a chance to answer but went on, 'Of *course* you haven't, and do you know why: because nobody'd fly in a plane with a captain who might be gawping at herself in the mirror when she ought to be watching the sky for other aircraft.'

'Oh shut *up*, Ned.' Jenna stirred her tea. 'Why should a woman gawp at herself and a man not? I've seen *you* in the bathroom, pulling your face about when you thought nobody was looking.'

'That's different. I'm zapping zits not admiring my beauty, breathtaking though it is.'

11

'Hooh!' whooped Jenna, 'you've a complexion like a cold pizza, you donkey.'

'Jenna!' scowled Mum. 'Ned can't help having spots, it's his age, and it's cruel of you to mock.'

'What about him mocking me, just because I said I'm going to be an airline captain. Isn't that just as cruel?'

'No, dear, it isn't. Ned's mocking a *choice* of yours, whereas he has no choice in the matter of his complexion.'

'So what do *you* think about my choice, Mum? You haven't said.'

Her mother smiled. 'I think possibly it's a passing fancy, darling, brought on by yesterday's flight home from Malaga. You could change your mind a hundred times before you leave school.'

'You didn't say that to *him* when he said he was going to be a millionaire.'

'That's because Ned didn't ask me what I thought, Jenna.' She smiled. '*Everybody* wants to be a millionaire. Few succeed, and I suspect that's also true of those who dream of flying.'

'It isn't a dream,' muttered Jenna. 'Not with me. I *know* I'll fly. I've always known.'

'Drink your tea, sweetheart,' said her father through a mouthful of scone, 'and don't contradict your mother.'

Two

Jenna at five, going to school by herself for the very first time. Ned's supposed to be keeping an eye on her but he's nearly eight and has his own fish to fry. He's way out in front with his best friend Andrew Scholes, crossing West Lane towards the museum car park. Jenna is trotting, trying to catch up. West Lane is busy, he's supposed to see her across. She steps off the kerb, calling to him. Luckily she's hit a lull in the traffic, crosses unharmed, hurries on plump legs up the incline. The two boys are halfway across the car park, barely in sight. She's about to call out again when something on the pavement catches her eye. A shape, etched on a flagstone. Jenna recognizes the shape as a plane, like the one in her alphabet book. There's a word too, but she doesn't know what it says because she can't read. Maybe it says P for plane, same as the book. When she looks up, Ned and Andrew have gone.

She toddles across the damp asphalt, sees the steps she climbed yesterday with Mum. That's the way to school, the way the boys must have gone. She climbs the steps. At the top is a lumpy road. It goes both ways. No boys. Which way did they go? Which way did Mum go yesterday? Jenna doesn't know.

She's trailing along the lumpy road under dripping trees,

grizzling, when a woman comes out of a doorway and looks at her. 'What's the matter, lovey, lost your mam?'

'Ned's left me,' sniffles Jenna. 'I don't know the way to school.'

'Well, no need to be all upset, lovey. Here.' She mops Jenna's cheeks with a tissue, tells her to blow hard. 'I'm going right past the school so we'll walk together, shall we?'

And so it's all right. At hometime Ned's waiting for her, holds her hand all the way. He's had a telling-off from the head teacher for leaving her but Jenna doesn't know this, and by the time they get home she's forgotten the incident; forgotten how frightened she's been. The only bit she remembers is the plane on the flagstone and the word, which might be P for plane.

Three

Next day was Saturday. 'Where are you going, dear?' asked Mum as Jenna shrugged into her jacket.

'Library,' said Jenna, 'to find out how you get to be a pilot.'

'If you wait an hour or so, Dad's taking the car into Keeley. He could drop you off.' Haverham was too small to have its own library so Keeley was where villagers went to borrow books.

Jenna shook her head. 'It's OK, Mum, I'll get the bus. Dad'd want me in and out of the library in five minutes, then drag me round Staples for about six hours looking at scanners.'

'I don't know why you're bothering,' growled Ned. He was sitting at the table in his dressing-gown, nursing a mug of coffee. 'I told you, there are no women airline captains.' He looked at his mother. 'Are there, Mum?'

She shook her head. 'I don't know, Ned. I don't think we've flown with one, and I can't remember ever seeing one at an airport, but that doesn't mean there aren't any. Anyway,' she smiled brightly, 'Jenna's following up an interest and that's always a good thing, even if the interest doesn't last.'

It was still early when Jenna got to Keeley. The library had just opened and there was no queue at the inquiry desk. The assistant looked up. 'How may I help you?'

'I'm . . . I want to find out how people get to be pilots.'

'Fly planes, you mean?'

'Yes.'

'OK, you want the reference section, sports and hobbies. That's the seven-nineties.' She pointed. 'Up this aisle, eighth fixture on the left. Come back if you need help.'

Jenna frowned, walking up the aisle counting fixtures. Didn't sound right, sports and hobbies. It's not a sport, flying an Airbus. Not a hobby either.

The seven-nineties were near the floor. She squatted, reading spines. There were rows and rows of stuff she didn't want: abseiling, bungee-jumping, camping, canoeing – every sport in the world except flying. She was ready to give up and go back to the desk when her eyes came to rest on a battered spine which had once been white and blue. She could hardly make out the title, but it looked like *The Air Pilot's Manual – Flying Training*. She slid it out, flicked through. It was in sections, with diagrams showing instrument panels and planes with various parts labelled. Aileron. Flap. Rudder. The only snag was, it seemed to be about *little* planes: two-seaters. *That's probably why it's under sports*, she thought.

She searched a bit further but there was nothing about airliners, so she straightened up and took the manual to the desk. The young woman smiled. 'Find what you wanted?'

Jenna nodded. 'Sort of, except it's about small planes and I want to fly big ones. You know: jumbos and that.'

'Ah yes, but you see . . .' The woman smiled. 'I think you'll find all pilots learn to fly small planes first, then go on to bigger ones.'

16

'Oh, OK, I'll take this one.'

'You can't take it out, love, it's reference only. You can sit at one of the tables and read it, take notes. And we can photocopy pages for you if you like.'

'Oh – thanks. I'll stay a bit and read.' She pulled a face. 'Should've brought a notebook.'

She sat down at half past nine, and when she looked up she was surprised to find that it was nearly a quarter past eleven. She returned the manual to the desk and left the library, her head full of strange new words and phrases. Turn and bank. Straight and level. Upper air work. Her state was a mixture of yearning, excitement and determination. 'I'll fly,' she whispered to herself. 'I'll fly, whatever Ned says. Whatever *anybody* says.' She smiled. 'Eh, aeroplane stone?' She hardly noticed the busride home, and nearly missed her stop.

four

One morning not long after her sixth birthday, Jenna walks up the slope towards the car park, glancing as she always does at the aeroplane stone. This time something's different. Something's changed. It isn't the stone and it isn't the little plane. The word's the same too, except . . .

I'm reading it! A—M—Y. Amye. Amye. She frowns. What does amye mean? I know: I'll ask Mrs Barton. She'll know. Mrs Barton knows everything. Jenna no longer needs her brother to show her the way to school. She hurries on.

'Miss.'

'What is it, Jenna?'

'Miss, what does amye mean?'

'Amye?' The teacher frowns. 'Spell it out please, Jenna.'

'Miss, it's A—M—Y.'

'A—M—Y spells Amy, Jenna. It's a girl's name.'

'It's . . . my mum's called Amy, miss. I didn't know you spelt it like that.'

Miss Barton smiles. 'That's how it's spelt, Jenna. Why don't you write it in your spellings book, under A?'

'Yes, miss.'

Jenna doesn't understand why her mother's name is on the aeroplane stone. She suspects magic comes into it somewhere because the aeroplane stone is magic. She never forgets to glance at it when passing. If it needs attention because there's a twig or leaf or toffee-paper on it, she'll scrape the debris with the side of her shoe onto an adjoining flag, taking care not to step on the stone itself. She must never, ever tread on the aeroplane stone or something terrible will happen to her mother. A rhyme comes into her head:

> Step on the plane
> Give your mother pain.

She hasn't a clue where this couplet comes from, but she's in absolutely no doubt it means what it says.

Five

Sunday breakfast. Amy Finch cleared Ned and Jenna's cereal bowls and said, 'It would be nice if the two of you would call in at Grandad's sometime today. I'd go myself if I hadn't promised Dad I'd go to the garden centre with him.'

Ned shook his head. 'I can't, I'm meeting Gavin down the mall.'

Peter Finch glanced up from his newspaper. 'Gavin? Who's Gavin, Ned?'

'Gavin Lassiter, lad at school. His folks moved here last term.'

'He's a big bully,' said Jenna. 'Ned's the only one who bothers with him.'

'No I'm not,' protested Ned. 'Gav's got loads of friends.'

'Huh! *Gav* pulled Sarah Lipton off her chair in I.T. because there wasn't a computer free.'

'No he didn't. He wouldn't.'

'Well he did, so there.'

'Whoa!' Their father frowned. 'No fratching at the breakfast table, please.' He looked at Ned. 'What time are you meeting this Gavin character?'

'Half ten.'

'Hmmm – bit early to be popping in on your grandad beforehand.' His eyes switched to Jenna. 'What about you, sweetheart? No pressing engagements, have you?'

'I . . . thought I'd sign on the Internet, Dad, look for stuff about learning to fly.'

'Yes, but you can do that any time. Your grandad's lonely now that he hasn't got Grandma, and I know he'd like it if you dodged round to say hello. You needn't stay – just hello Grandad, how you doing, and away.'

Jenna gazed at her upside-down reflection in the teaspoon. 'I know, Dad, but he's . . . different. I mean he was always laughing, cracking corny jokes. Now he just sits in the chair staring at the carpet. I never know what to say.'

'Tell him about Nerja,' suggested her mother. 'How hot it was, what a lovely time we all had. Show him your tan, say there'll be some snapshots in a week or so. Your grandad's depressed, darling, that's why he's different with you. You don't have to be different with him. Be your cheerful chatty self. He'll snap out of it in time.'

Jenna nodded glumly. 'All right I'll go, but I don't think it's fair. If *I* have to, why not Ned? He always gets to do what he likes.'

'No I don't,' retorted her brother. 'I have to live with you for a start.'

'That's enough, Ned,' snapped his father. 'One more word out of you and you'll go with Jenna no matter who's waiting for you down the mall.'

Breakfast over, Jenna went up to her room to get ready. She loved her grandad but his house didn't feel the same without Grandma, plus he had cried the last time she had gone to

21

see him. There's nothing more embarrassing than someone old crying, because what're you supposed to do? You can't dab an old guy's face with a tissue and say blow, and you can't tell him it'll be all right because it won't be. *Should've promised to meet somebody down the mall*, she thought, *same as Ned*.

Six

''Lo Grandad.'

'Oh it's you, Jenna. Come on in then.' The old man turned and shuffled along the dim hallway.

Jenna shut the door in the sun's face and followed, wondering how soon she could leave without seeming rude. The house had a smell she'd never noticed when Grandma was alive.

'Now then.' His smile was watery as he nodded towards a rumpled armchair. 'Sit down while I put the kettle on. You'll have a cup of tea, won't you?'

Jenna nodded. 'Yes, thanks, Grandad.' She didn't want tea, she wanted to be out of this sad house, but a cup and saucer would give her hands something to do while she told him about Nerja.

While Grandad rattled and clinked in the kitchen she gazed around the room. It had all the same things in it that it had had before Grandma died but it was different in a number of ways. The cushions weren't plumped for one thing. There were linty bits all over the Afghan rug and dust lay thickly in a splash of sunlight on the sideboard, which had a beaker on it with streaks where coffee had dribbled down. Grandma would've had a fit if she'd found a beaker on her teak sideboard.

'Here we are then.' He stooped stiffly to put the tray on the low coffee table. 'Milk and sugar, isn't it?'

'Milk,' said Jenna, 'no sugar, thanks.'

'Right.' He poured tea, gave her hers, sat down with his. 'Nice holiday?' His tone suggested an effort to be polite rather than genuine interest.

Jenna nodded. 'Terrific, thanks. Nine days of sunshine, not a cloud in the sky.'

'Very nice. What was the name of the place again?'

'Nerja.'

'Oh, yes. Costa del Sol isn't it?'

'Yes.'

He nodded, sipped his tea and lapsed into the silence she'd dreaded, staring at the rug.

'We went on an excursion, Grandad. Granada.'

'Huh?' He looked up, frowning. 'Oh, Granada you say. Famous, that. Old song about it.' For a ghastly moment she thought he was going to sing, but he resumed his rug-gazing instead.

'One night this giant creepy-crawly flew through our window. A cicada, size of a sparrow.'

'Hmmm.' Without looking up, the old man nodded. 'We'd things like that in Palestine, Jenna. Lads used to put 'em on bits of string, fly 'em like kites.'

'Talking of flying, Grandad, *I* want to fly.'

'Eh?' His head came up. 'How d'you mean, fly?'

'I mean, be a pilot. Airline captain.'

'Ah.' He lifted his cup and drank, studying her over the rim. 'What brought this on, Jenna?'

She shrugged. 'I've always wanted to fly, Grandad, but it was listening to the captain on the flight home

24

that put airliners into my head.'

'I see. Told your mum, have you?'

'Yes.'

'And?'

Jenna pulled a face. 'A passing fancy, she calls it. Dad think so too, and as for Ned . . .'

Grandad arched his brow. 'What about Ned?'

'Oh, you know what Ned's like, Grandad. Says nobody'd fly with a captain who'd be admiring herself in the mirror instead of keeping a lookout . . . stuff like that.'

'Ha!' The old man set down his cup hard enough to slop tea in the saucer. 'I bet he's never heard of Amy Johnson then.'

Jenna looked at him. For the first time in months there was a light in her grandfather's eyes. For the first time in months he seemed to be interested in what she was saying. She pressed on. 'I've never heard of her either, Grandad. Who is she?'

'Was,' the old man corrected. 'Who *was* she. More tea, lovey?'

'N . . . no thanks. Amy Johnson?'

'Yes. Amy Johnson was a pilot, Jenna, back in the Thirties when flying was still a bit of a novelty. I was younger than you are now, and Amy was my hero. Heroine, I suppose I should say. D'you know what a biplane is?'

'No.'

'No, well you don't see 'em much now. A biplane's got two sets of wings, one above the other, with struts between.'

'Oh, yes.' Jenna nodded. 'I know what you mean. I've seen 'em in movies, they had them in World War One, right?'

'That's right, Jenna. They were flimsy, all wood and canvas, and in 1930 Amy Johnson flew one all the way to Australia. She was the first woman ever to make that flight

25

solo and the papers were full of her for weeks. I went to the pictures and saw her on a newsreel, landing at Darwin.'

Jenna heard the break in her grandfather's voice and saw tears in his eyes, but it wasn't like last time. She'd read about people crying with happiness and it had always seemed daft to her, but something like that was happening to Grandad as he talked about his heroine. She put down her cup and saucer. 'I'm just off to the bathroom, Grandad, but I want to ask you something when I come back.'

The old man nodded. 'Ask me anything you like.' He pulled a large handkerchief from his pocket, lifted his glasses and dabbed at his eyes. 'I'm glad you dropped in this morning, lovey – you've done me a power of good.'

She went upstairs and along the landing. The bedroom door stood open and she glanced in. Under the pink lamp on the bedside unit was a gun.

Seven

Over lunch Mum said, 'How was Grandad, Jenna? Any more cheerful?'

Jenna nodded. 'Not at first, but he got really interested when I told him what I want to do.'

'What d'you mean, sweetheart, want to do?'

'You know – fly planes.'

'Oh, *Jenna.*' Dad put down his fork. 'You didn't go bothering your grandad with *that*, surely?'

'Yes I did,' scowled Jenna. 'I had to talk about something or we'd have sat there like two dummies, same as last time. And like I said, he was really interested.'

Her father looked at her. 'How interested?'

'Well, he told me stuff about when he was my age. How he used to be an Amy Johnson fan.'

'Who did *she* sing with?' asked Ned through a mouthful of crusty roll.

'She was a pilot, you turkey,' spat Jenna, 'a pioneer aviatrix.'

'Hooo!' hooted Ned. '*Aviatrix.* Swallowed a dictionary have you, Sis?'

'Be quiet, Ned,' growled Dad. 'Go on, Jenna.'

'He said Mum's called Amy because of Amy Johnson. He wanted to be a pilot but he couldn't, so he and Grandma called Mum Amy after his heroine. *And* he carved Amy's plane and name on a flagstone.'

Mum nodded. 'I remember that. He showed it to me once, when I was little. And I know I was named after her, but I never knew he wanted to be a pilot himself.' She looked at Jenna. 'So he seemed interested?'

Jenna nodded. 'Yes. He mentioned some place – a museum near Bridlington that's got all Amy Johnson's stuff in it, medals and that. Says he'll take me there.'

'And will you go?'

She shrugged. 'Dunno. I mean come *on* – I'm nearly fourteen. You grow out of going around with your grandad, know what I mean?'

'You didn't *tell* him that?'

'*Would* I, Mum? I said we'd have to fix it or something.'

'Good, because it sounds to me as though Grandad might be coming out of this depression he's been in since Grandma died. Your dad and I have been worried sick about him, you know. Even suspected him of considering suicide.'

'What?' Jenna looked at her mother, who pulled a face.

'Well it happens, sweetheart. Widowers, they have been known to . . .'

'There was a gun . . .'

'A gun? *Where?* At Grandad's?'

Jenna nodded. 'By his bed. I saw it when I went to the loo.'

'Oh God!' She looked at her husband. 'D'you think we'd better get round there, Peter?'

He shrugged, looked at Jenna. 'Are you *sure* it was a gun, sweetheart? Did you mention to Grandad that you'd seen it?'

'Oh yes,' Jenna nodded, 'it was a gun. I mentioned it and he said, "Oh, that: that's nothing, just a little souvenir I picked up in Palestine." Then he went upstairs and I think he put it away somewhere, because when he came back he sort of rubbed his hands together and said "*There*", as if that was done with. He was smiling.'

'Hmmm.' Peter Finch glanced at his wife. 'Did you know your dad had a gun, Amy?'

She nodded. 'Yes, but I'd forgotten. Mum was always on at him to hand it in – you know, when they have these amnesties – but he always put it off. Said it might come in handy for burglars.'

'What sort is it?' This from Ned.

His mother shook her head. 'Don't ask me, I know nothing about guns. Some sort of revolver, I think. It was kept well out of my reach.'

'Where?'

'*I* don't know, Ned. Whatever does it matter?'

The boy shrugged. 'Just curious.'

'Well.' Dad stirred his tea. 'From what Jenna says, it doesn't sound as if the old man means to shoot himself in the immediate future.' He smiled. 'Not when he's planning an excursion to the seaside with his little granddaughter.'

Mum nodded. 'Yes, that's good isn't it? He's always been so good with the children, I think perhaps he's getting back to normal.'

'Don't forget your bucket and spade, Sis,' sneered Ned.

Eight

Jenna, seven years old on a warm Saturday at Grandad's
allotment. She's often here on Saturdays while Mum and
Grandma shop in Keeley and Ned helps Dad with jobs round
the house. Today Grandad hoes carefully between dead-straight
rows of beetroot while Jenna picks caterpillars off the
nasturtiums and drops them in a jam jar. She enjoys the work
because Grandad resents the way the caterpillars make lace of
his nasturtium leaves and she likes to feel useful, but she'll stay
well away from the rain-barrel later when he shakes the
wretched creatures into the water like someone putting salt on
fish and chips.

In front of her as she squats, an untidy picket fence marks
the boundary between Grandad's allotment and the allotment
of old Rudyard. Rudyard doesn't do much with his patch of soil.
There's a clump of rhubarb and some scrubby raspberry canes
but it's mostly grass and nettles because Rudyard isn't a
gardener, he's a pigeon fancier. His shed, which Grandad calls
a loft, stands against the overgrown privet hedge which divides
Rudyard's patch from the next. The old man is deeply
unpopular with his fellow allotment holders because his weeds
launch seeds on little parachutes to land on their well-hoed

tilth, and because his pigeons grow plump on the currants they grow. Jenna quite likes him though, and he always seems pleased to see her, perhaps because hers is the only smile he sees.

Now as she squats absorbed, Rudyard's flock launches itself in a clatter of iridescent quills and swerves in front of the sun so that its shadow flits across her face. The child looks up, shielding her eyes with a hand. The birds swoop in tight formation low over the loft where the old man stands watching, then beat strongly southwards, gaining height. Surprised by a soaring exultation she feels as an ache, Jenna straightens up and stands open-mouthed, following with her eyes. It's me, she murmurs somewhere in her head, it's me, me up there. The feeling fades as the flock recedes, merging with the blue, and Jenna will never experience it again, but she'll know for the rest of her life, deep down, what kites and pigeons are for.

Nine

It's always a bummer, first day back at school. To Jenna the Easter break felt to have flown, probably because the Finches had jetted off to Spain, returning only last Thursday. There was one good thing about this chilly Monday morning though, and its name was Matty Brewster.

Matty was Jenna's best friend. She lived halfway down Main Street and had waited in her doorway every morning since they were both six so that they could walk to school together. She was there now, watching her friend approach.

'Hi, Jen, you look really brown.'

'So how come I feel blue?'

Matty laughed, falling into step. 'The words *school* and *rotten* spring to mind.'

'That'd be right. What have you been up to?'

'Nothing spectacular. Hanging round the mall in the drizzle, thinking about you playing frisbee on a golden beach with two drop-dead gorgeous waiters.'

'Hooo – fat chance with *my* dad about. Booting a ball around with Ned more like. It was OK though – wish I was still there.'

'Oh, right. Didn't miss *me* then.'

''Course I did, I don't mean that. I mean I wish we were *both* there, just the two of us.'

'*And* those waiters.'

'Oh yes, goes without saying.'

They crossed Rawdon Road with the lollipop lady, joined the uniformed throng dawdling down Butt Lane. 'I did half expect you'd call Saturday,' said Matty.

Jenna nodded. 'I know. Sorry. I had to get to the library, read up on flying.' She told Matty about her ambition and her family's reaction to it.

Matty scowled. 'Tell 'em to take a running jump. *I* would. It's not like you've decided to be a bullfighter or a professional bungee-jumper or something. There's nothing daft about wanting to be an airline captain, so go for it.'

Jenna reached for her friend's hand, squeezed it. 'I knew *you'd* back me up, Mat, even though I *didn't* call you on Saturday.' As they turned into the schoolyard holding hands a boy jeered, 'When's the wedding?'

'Right after your funeral, corpse-features,' cried Matty. The boy flushed as his companions guffawed. The two girls linked arms and walked on, noses in the air.

Ten

'Hey Jen, why don't you have a word with old Worldwide, ask him if he knows any good Internet sites for budding flyers?' It was morning break, breezy but dry. Matty and Jenna were strolling round the perimeter of the all-weather pitch.

Jenna nodded. 'Good idea, Mat, thanks.'

Lunchtime she went along to the I.T. suite. Worldwide's real name was Mr Webb and he was there as usual, peering into a screen. Jenna cleared her throat so he'd know she was there. He looked up.

'Yes, Jenna Finch?'

'I . . . I need to find out about training as an airline pilot and I wondered if you knew any sites I should visit.'

He swivelled his seat, looked at her. 'Airline pilot? Is this a serious career choice Jenna, or are you researching a project?'

'It's what I want to be, sir.'

'Hmmm. Hard road, young woman. Bags and bags of study. How's your trig?'

Jenna pulled a face. Trigonometry didn't figure in her top ten subjects. 'I get through it, sir, just about.'

The teacher shook his head. 'Won't do I'm afraid, Jenna.

Aim to become a trig genius. A prodigy. The Robbie Williams of trigonometry.'

'Robbie Williams, sir?'

'Well.' He shrugged. 'Whoever. Navigation you see, map-reading. Trig's essential if you want to avoid flying into mountains and things.' He smiled. 'Trig apart, there's an excellent CD Rom you might want to check out. *Flight Simulator 98*, or there might be an updated version by now. Have you got Windows at home?'

'Yes.'

'Fine. They'll have *Simulator* at PC World. I'm not sure how much it'll set you back but it won't break the bank, and among other things you can use it to practise landings at any decent-size airport in the world. I'd lend you mine if I hadn't passed it on to a nephew a couple of years back.'

Jenna shook her head. 'My dad'll get it for me sir, Saturday.'

'Lucky girl. See me at half-three and I'll suggest a site or two. And Jenna?'

She turned in the doorway. 'Sir?'

'Good luck.'

'That's *three*,' she whispered to herself as she hurried along the corridor, 'three people on my side. Grandad, Matty, and Worldwide Webb. Three for, three against so it's even. No it's *not*.' She grinned. 'There's *me*, so it's four against three, and that's a poem.' She whispered her poem over and over as she crossed the yard:

'There's me, there's me
It's four against three.'

OK so it wasn't Larkin, but it sure beat *Step on the plane, Give your mother pain* and that's what counts isn't it? Progress.

35

Eleven

Midnight. Jenna lay with her hands behind her head, staring at her bedroom ceiling. She'd spent the evening visiting the two websites Worldwide had tracked down for her and surfing for others. She'd gathered quite a bit of information, including the addresses of two colleges for trainee pilots. She'd composed the same letter to both of these requesting details, without revealing her age. She suspected they might ignore an inquiry from a kid. She hadn't told her parents what she was doing either, not wishing to encounter further discouragement.

Ned had barged in as she was sealing the second envelope, pretending to be hunting for a rubber band but really doing it just to annoy her. Jenna liked her own space and he knew it. She told him she had no rubber bands but he seemed reluctant to leave, drifting about the room picking things up and putting them down in the wrong places. When she mentioned this he said, 'Talking about things and their places, I wonder where Grandad keeps that gun you saw?' She told him she'd no idea and asked him to go but instead he leaned against the wall, hands in pockets, gazing out of her window.

'I'd have thought you'd have *some* idea from the noises he made upstairs. I mean, was he in his bedroom the whole time or did he go in the spare room, or even up to the loft?'

She'd spoken sharply then. 'I've *told* you I don't *know*. If you're so interested, go and ask Grandad but for goodness' sake leave me alone, I'm busy.' He'd left, scowling and muttering, but now she couldn't get to sleep for wondering why he'd asked about the gun.

Maybe he's thinking of pinching it so he can show off with it to that Gavin Lassiter. He'd be impressed with something like that, would Lassiter. She rolled onto her side and pulled the duvet up over her ear. *I should never have mentioned the flipping gun in Ned's hearing. I suppose I could try persuading Grandad to hand it in at the police station but what if he got mad, shouted that it was none of my business, lost interest in my plan to be a pilot? No, better leave it for now. It's probably nothing anyway, just Ned being Ned. He's a mega-pain but he's not a thief, so why can't I fall asl . . .*

Jenna slept.

Twelve

'Dad?' Tuesday breakfast.

'What is it, Jenna?' Peter Finch was running a bit late, Jenna detected a hint of impatience in his tone. *Oh-oh*, she thought, *tactical error*. No option but to press on. 'I talked to Mr Webb yesterday. He recommended a CD Rom, *Flight Simulator*. I was wondering if we could get it, Saturday.'

'Jenna.' Her father put down his coffee cup. 'It's nearly a quarter to eight, I've the Centre to open in sixteen minutes and you want to talk to me about shopping.' Peter Finch managed a mobile phone outlet in Keeley. 'Won't it keep till teatime?'

Jenna, relieved he hadn't stamped on the idea, nodded. 'Yes, Dad, sorry.'

'*Flight Simulator*?' Ned hadn't forgiven his sister for last night. 'Andrew's got *Flight Simulator*, it's crap.'

'Ned!' His mother frowned. 'I've told you before, I won't have that sort of language in this house. Use it with your friends if you must, but don't bring it home.'

Ned shrugged. 'Sorry, Mum.' Jenna stuck her tongue out at him but he pretended not to see. 'By the way, I'll be a few minutes late this aft. Thought I'd drop in on Grandad since I couldn't make it Sunday.'

Jenna gave him a sharp look. His expressionless face assumed a smarmy smile when his mother said, 'That's thoughtful, darling, give him my love.'

Jenna, furious, imitated his tone inside her head. *Thought I'd drop in on Grandad since I couldn't make it Sunday. Creep.* She was tempted to mention how he'd questioned her last night but she managed to bite her tongue. They'd only think she was getting back at him. Dad pushed back his chair and stood up and the moment passed.

She was worried though. When her father had gone and Ned was upstairs she said, 'Mum, has Grandad's gun got bullets?'

Mum was bent down loading the dishwasher. She shook her head. 'I've no idea, darling. Isn't it time you were getting ready?'

Thirteen

Friday. Amy Finch collected the holiday snaps from Boots on her way home from work. She was a sales assistant at M&S and Boots was on the same block. After tea she fished them out of her shopping bag. 'Who wants a look?'

Everybody did. They sat in a half-circle and went through them. There were the usual duds nobody could remember taking: a blurred shot from behind of total strangers leaning against a jetty-rail, a rash of pale flecks which might be gulls in flight, a seascape half obliterated by the photographer's thumb, but there were some good ones too. When they'd looked and she'd extracted the duds, Mum knocked the snapshots square, slipped them back in the wallet and handed them to Jenna. 'Your grandad'll enjoy looking at these, darling. You are calling round this evening, aren't you?'

Jenna nodded. Grandad had left a message on the answering machine, something about Bridlington. He'd asked her to call him back but she'd decided to bob across instead. He lived at Marsh, which meant a twenty-minute walk but the evening was fine, she'd phoned Matty to go with her and she wanted to tell the old man about the Internet sites and her letters to the two colleges. She'd another reason as well, which she was keeping to herself.

'Hi, Mat.'

Her friend was waiting by the bus-shelter which was otherwise deserted: Marsh had two buses a day and both were long gone.

'Hello, Biggles.' Matty had taken to calling Jenna Biggles after the hero of a flying story she'd read. Jenna would be furious if Ned called her that, but she didn't mind it from Matty. They strode side by side along the lane.

'How is your grandad,' asked Matty, 'now that . . . you know?' She'd met her friend's grandad several times, but not since the death of his wife.

'Oh . . .' Jenna shrugged, 'he's picking up I think. Better than a few weeks ago.'

'Good.' Matty smiled. 'He'll like the holiday snaps anyway. Can't wait to see 'em myself.'

Jenna pulled a face. 'They're no great shakes, Mat, just the usual boring stuff.'

'You mean you didn't get a shot of Manuel, the drop-dead gorgeous waiter?'

'Manuel's a mythical beast, Mat. Might as well ask if I got one of a mermaid.'

'*I* took one of a mermaid once, at Ingoldmells. Bit blurred, but . . .'

'Yeah, right.'

The old man had dragged a kitchen chair to his doorway and was sitting in the last of the sun. He squinted up at the two girls, shielding his eyes with a hand. 'Hello, Jenna, I thought you'd ring rather than walk all this way.' He got up stiffly.

'And you've brought your friend.' He smiled at Matty. 'Hatty, isn't it?'

'Matty, Mr Larwood.'

'Oh that's right, I remember now. Matty.' He picked up the chair. 'Just let me take this out of the way and we'll go inside, eh? Bit chilly once the sun's down.'

'Here, let me.' Jenna took the chair. 'I'll put the kettle on as well if that's all right.'

'''Course it's all right, it's lovely to see you both. Brought your holiday snaps, have you?'

'Oh yes, here.' She pulled them out of her jeans pocket. 'You and Matty check 'em out while I make a pot of tea.'

When she brought the tray the two were smiling over a shot of Amy Finch pulling a face over a plate of food. 'Yeah, Mum wasn't too keen on the calamari, Grandad.'

'Calamari?'

'Squid.'

'Ugh!' Matty shivered.

'No.' The old man shook his head. 'I wouldn't be either, foreign muck. Saw more than my share of that in Palestine.'

This mention of Palestine gave Jenna an unexpected opening. 'Grandad?'

'What, love?'

'Would you . . . can Matty see your souvenir of Palestine, please?'

He frowned. 'Souvenir?'

'Yes, *you know*.' She motioned with her head to indicate upstairs.

'Oh.' His face cleared. '*That*.' He shrugged. 'I suppose so if she wants to, but I hope you're not going round telling every Tom, Dick and Harry I've got a gun, Jenna. I could end up in clink, you know.'

Jenna nodded. 'I know, Grandad, I hadn't even mentioned it to Matty, but I know she'd love to see it.'

'Yes, all right.' He levered himself out of the armchair and shuffled out of the room.

Matty hissed, 'Gun? I'm not bothered about seeing a *gun*, Jen. Why'd you tell him . . .?'

'Ssssh!' Jenna shook her head. 'Something I had to find out, Mat. I'll tell you later.'

They sat without speaking as the old man moved about upstairs. Jenna knew Matty was mad at her. She hoped she'd forgive her once she'd explained.

Footfalls on the stairs. Jenna turned. Her grandad stood in the doorway looking troubled.

'What's up, Grandad?' she murmured, though she already knew the answer.

'It's gone,' he croaked. 'Somebody must've got into the house and pinched the flipping gun.'

Fourteen

'What you gonna *do*, Grandad?' Before, Jenna had relished the prospect of Ned in trouble. She'd not thought it through because deep down she hadn't believed the gun would be missing. Faced with the fact of its disappearance she found herself deeply reluctant to incriminate her brother, and this surprised her.

'Nay,' the old man shook his head. 'I don't know, love. I can hardly call the police, can I?'

Matty frowned. 'Is anything else missing, Mr Larwood?'

'I don't think so, Hatty, and that's what worries me most. It's as if whoever did this *knew* the gun was here and came specially to get it.'

'They didn't *break* in,' said Matty, 'or there'd be damage of some sort. That means whoever it was must have walked in. D'you go out leaving your door unlocked, Mr Larwood?'

He shook his head again. 'Never, Hatty. Not on purpose anyway. I suppose it's possible I might have forgotten the odd time, but that doesn't explain why they didn't take anything else, does it? I mean there's the video, TV, radio, microwave oven – all stuff burglars go for, and they didn't touch any of it. They *must*'ve come for the gun, but how the heck did they know it was here?' He looked at Jenna. 'Are you absolutely *sure* you haven't told anybody, love?'

'I mentioned it to Mum and Dad.'

'Nobody else?'

'No.' She could have told him Ned was there when she mentioned the gun, but she chose not to. Getting your pain of a brother shouted at or grounded is fair enough, he'd do the same for you. Getting him arrested is quite different. *I'll confront him*, she thought. *If he puts it back where he found it without Grandad knowing, maybe it'll be all right.*

'You see,' murmured the old man half to himself, 'whoever swiped that gun didn't take it to sell, they'd have got more for the video, so they must've wanted it for something else. A crime. And if it's used in a crime – if somebody gets shot – and the men are caught and tell where they got the gun, I'm for the high-jump, as well as having some poor beggar's death on my conscience.'

'Maybe it wasn't for a crime,' suggested Jenna. 'Some people collect guns, all sorts of weapons. Could've been somebody like that, couldn't it?'

''T'isn't likely love – collectors *buy* items for their collections, they don't pinch them.' He sighed. 'I should've listened to your grandma, Jenna. She told me a dozen times to hand the damned thing in but I wouldn't, and now look. Anyway.' He shrugged, lowered himself into an armchair. 'It's my problem and I'll have to think about it, decide what's best to do. In the meantime there's this trip to Brid.' He looked at Matty. 'Perhaps you'd like to come too, eh Hatty?'

fifteen

'So,' probed Matty as she and Jenna walked back down Marsh Lane, 'what was it you had to find out, and did you find it?'

Jenna shook her head. 'It was nothing, Mat, it doesn't matter.'

'You said you'd tell me later.'

'I will.'

'I thought *later* meant when we're by ourselves.'

'No, it meant later.'

'Well, it was obviously about your grandad's gun. I think you knew it'd be missing.'

'Listen, Mat.' Jenna took her friend's arm, drew her to a halt and looked her in the eye. 'You're my best friend, always have been, and I don't like keeping secrets from you, but just this time I've got to ask you to trust me. Something awful might be happening, but it's a family thing and I don't want it to go outside the family at the moment. You do understand, don't you?'

Matty shrugged. 'I suppose so, Jen, but like . . . if you're in some sort of trouble, can't I help? It's what friends are for.'

'I know Mat, and I'd love to have your help, but the way

things are at the moment there's really nothing you can do.' She smiled. 'There might be later though, if we're still friends by then.'

Matty gave Jenna's hand a squeeze. ''Course we'll still be friends, you turkey. If you're gonna be a whatsit . . . pioneer aviatrix, you'll need somebody with both feet on the ground while you've got your head in the clouds.'

Jenna returned the squeeze. 'Thanks, Mat, I mean it, and thanks for saying you'll come to Brid with me and Grandad on Sunday.' She grinned. 'Not the coolest way to spend a weekend, going to the seaside with your grandad, but it'll be a hundred times more fun with you there and it could even turn out to be dangerous, the state of Grandad's ancient Micra.'

Just hope I can stop thinking about that gun for a day.

Sixteen

Jenna got home just as the light was fading. Her mother was in the kitchen, ironing. She smiled. 'How's Grandad, darling?'

'Seems fine.' *Hope he doesn't phone about the gun.*

'Did he enjoy the snaps?'

'I think so, especially you and the calamari. Foreign muck, he called it when I told him it was squid.'

Mum nodded. 'Like father, like daughter. I suppose I'm only fit to take my holidays in Skegness or somewhere.'

Jenna grinned. 'Fine, as long as you don't mind the rest of us going off to Spain.'

'Charming. Did you fix a date for Bridlington?'

'Yes, Sunday.'

'*This* Sunday?'

'Sure, why not? Matty's coming too.'

'I hope you didn't *push* Grandad into going this Sunday and taking Matty along, Jenna.'

'*Would* I, Mum? He had it all worked out, and he *invited* Matty.'

'That's all right, then.'

'Dad out, is he?'

'Yes, he popped down to the Old White Lion for an hour.'
She smiled. 'Two hours ago.'

'Uh-huh, and what about Ned?' She made it sound casual.

'In his room playing computer games. *Don't* go disturbing
him, d'you hear? I'm tired and I can't do with the two of you
fratching.'

'I never hassle him unless he hassles *me*, Mum.' *Got to
talk to him though, got to* know. She hung her top over the
banister, went upstairs.

Her brother's door was closed. She could hear FX. She
knocked softly. No response. She knocked a bit harder,
hoping Mum wouldn't hear. This time a voice growled,
'What?'

'It's me, got to talk to you.'

'What about?'

'Oh come *on*, Ned, it's important.'

'It better be.' He opened the door a crack. 'What?'

'I've come from Grandad's.'

He sighed. 'And?'

'You *know* – what I told Mum and Dad about, last Sunday.'
She watched his face, which betrayed only irritation. He
shook his head. 'Look, Sis, I don't know what you're on
about and I'm busy.' He stepped back, started to close the
door.

'The gun.'

'Gun?' The crack widened again. 'What about the gun?'

'It's gone, Ned. Somebody pinched it, but then you knew
that already, right?'

'Huh?' He scowled. 'What're you *saying*, Jenna? How the
heck would I know a thing like that?'

'You asked about it, Mum then me. You were interested.'

He sneered. 'You're interested in *flying* but you haven't
nicked a Boeing seven-o-seven.'

Jenna glanced towards the stairs. Mum could come up any minute with a stack of ironed clothes. She looked at her brother. '*Have* you got it, Ned? I promise I won't tell. You can take it back, put it where you found it, nobody'll know.'

'Listen, Sis,' hissed Ned, 'for the last time, I'm *not* a thief, I *haven't* got Grandad's flipping gun and I *have* got better things to do than stand here listening to you all night, so why don't you go to your room, switch on your computer and play at being a pioneer flipping aviatrix.' He slammed the door.

As Jenna turned away her mother came to the foot of the stairs and called up. 'Jenna, I hope you're not bothering Ned after I asked you specially.'

'It's OK, Mum.' She crossed the landing, shut herself in her room and sat on the bed. She'd hoped to surprise her brother, see guilt on his face so she could make him take the gun back to Grandad's but it hadn't worked. He hadn't looked guilty at all. *Maybe that's because he hasn't got it*, she thought, but it was hard to believe. Who else knew about the gun? Nobody. Grandad was sure to get round to thinking about Ned's visit eventually, then what? The old guy wasn't daft. He was bound to wonder. And what if he told Mum Jenna was there when he discovered the weapon was missing? Mum'd wonder why she hadn't mentioned the matter when she got home, wouldn't she? It was a mess, and worse still it was a mess of Jenna's own making. *If I'd not seen the thing on the bedside table, or seen it and not mentioned it, or if I'd mentioned it to Grandad but not to Mum and Dad, none of this would be happening.* Jenna felt tired suddenly, but she knew there'd be little sleep for her that night.

Seventeen

Peter Finch looked at Jenna across the breakfast table. 'Are we still off to PC World, sweetheart, or have you had second thoughts?'

'She can't have had second thoughts 'cause she hasn't had her *first* one yet,' sniped Ned.

'Oh *I*'ve got my thoughts, Ned,' returned Jenna softly, 'and you know what they're about.'

Her brother lowered his eyes at once, started fiddling with his knife.

Their father noticed the boy's discomfiture and turned to Jenna. 'What *are* they about, Jenna?'

Jenna shook her head. 'Nothing, Dad, just sort of an ongoing discussion Ned and I are having. And yes, we *are* off to PC World if that's all right.'

'It's all right as long as it's just you and me. I don't fancy listening to this ongoing discussion all the way into Keeley.'

'It's OK, Dad,' mumbled Ned, 'I'm not off to Keeley anyway.'

PC World had stacks of *Flight Simulator*. Jenna slid one off the top and they queued at the checkout. 'Can we go straight home?' asked Jenna. 'I can't wait to get on this.'

51

''Fraid not, sweetheart. Your mum wants a few bits from Asda and I promised to call in at work, but it'll be quicker if you'll do Asda while I pop along to the Centre. How about that?'

'OK.'

Asda and PC World were parts of the same complex and the Cellphone Centre was a short walk away, so they stowed the software out of sight in the boot, left the car where it was and split up.

Asda was packed. Jenna set off up the first aisle, steering the trolley with one hand, clutching the list Dad had given her in the other. There were nine items on the list. She worked quickly, swerving her trolley through the Saturday morning throng. Within eight minutes of leaving the checkout at PC World she was queuing at another.

This took longer than it need have, because some shoppers seemed not to realize till they were halfway through packing that you have to *pay*. They'd be stuffing items into carrier-bags from a jumbled heap, and when the checkout girl called out the total they'd be like, 'Oh, just a minute, love,' and start fumbling in handbags or patting pockets for a purse or wallet. Having found it they'd pull out their credit card, loyalty card and a wad of dog-eared coupons, slap them on the counter for the girl to sort and go back to their packing. *Why*, mused Jenna, not for the first time, *don't they get everything ready while they're waiting in the queue, put it on the counter in a neat stack and concentrate on packing?* Incredible.

She was three from the front when she noticed Ned's unpleasant friend, Gavin Lassiter. He was slouching against the wall near Customer Services with his hands in his pockets, apparently eyeing up checkout girls. When he saw Jenna he treated her to a slow smile he probably thought looked sardonic, used his tongue to transfer the match he was chewing from one corner of his mouth to the other and looked away. Jenna hoped he wouldn't approach her when she left. In his one term at Haverham, Lassiter had earned almost everyone's dislike and she was at a loss to understand what Ned saw in him.

She needn't have worried. By the time she got through, Lassiter had moved further up the line and was chatting to a Saturday shelf-stacker she recognized vaguely from school. She left the store and set off across the car park, hoping Dad would be waiting by the Volvo.

Eighteen

Installing *Flight Simulator* was a lot harder than she'd expected. It seemed to take ages, clicking and whirring, giving her a box to type her name in, an ID number of twenty digits and some quick choices to make. Hands creeping round a clockface showed percentage of installation completed, only it wasn't a clock but something called an air speed indicator. She'd to register by phone, which Dad helped her with, and when the program was finally up and running she found herself staring at the instrument panel of a Cessna Skylane while some American guy told her she could take off as soon as she was ready.

Take off? He's got to be joking.

'Da-ad?' She twisted round in her seat.

Her father shrugged. 'Don't look at *me*, sweetheart, you're the one wants to fly.'

'*This lesson will end if you don't take off soon,*' said the invisible instructor. Jenna thought he sounded sarcastic.

'What shall I *do*?' she screeched. '*I* don't know how to take off.'

'Take it *easy*, sweetheart,' chuckled Dad, 'it's not *real*. You're here in your room, not sitting on the runway at Meigs

54

Field, wherever that is. Selecting HELP will zap that impatient Yank *and* point you to some essential reading. I think you need to know which keys control the plane, and what all those clocks on the dashboard are for.'

Jenna hit HELP and slumped with a sigh. 'It's a heck of a lot more complicated than I expected, Dad. What was that *other* voice quacking about, behind the instructor?'

'Weather report I think. Windspeed, cloudbase, that sort of thing.'

'You mean I'm supposed to take all that in *and* get the flipping plane off the ground?'

Her father nodded. 'I expect so, Jenna, yes.' He smiled. 'If being a pilot was easy, there'd be as many planes in the sky as there are cars on the motorway. In fact come to think of it, there might be no cars on the motorway at all.'

Jenna smiled too, but she felt more like bursting into tears. *I panicked. Amy Johnson flew all the way to Australia by herself and I panicked on a simulator in my bedroom. Maybe I should pack this stuff up, take it back to PC World, get my dosh back. Maybe Ned was right.*

'No, he wasn't.'

'*Who* wasn't, sweetheart?'

She hadn't meant to speak out loud, shook her head. 'Nobody, Dad, I was practising talking to myself, ready for when I fly solo to Australia.'

Nineteen

'I'll fly solo,' said Grandad. 'You two sit in the back so you can chat.' Half-eight Sunday morning, bright except when a stiff breeze blew rags of cloud across the sun. Matty and Jenna belted up in the back seat while the old man, smartly dressed for the first time since his wife's funeral, started the engine and fussed with his mirrors. 'Chocks away,' he joked as the car rolled forward. Jenna smiled, not because it was a particularly funny joke but because it was his first for a while.

The roads weren't busy yet. They were in no rush so Albert Larwood took the scenic route, steering the old Micra between green hedges and up over stretches of bleakly beautiful moorland while Jenna made Matty laugh with the story of her first simulated flight.

'That wasn't a *flight*,' hooted her friend when she'd finished. 'It was a simulated stay-on-the-ground. If you were a *bird* you'd be a flipping penguin.'

'Flipping sort of *goes* with penguin, doesn't it,' said Jenna inconsequentially, wishing she felt as light-hearted as she sounded. In fact she was still dejected by what had happened yesterday, and made a determined effort to drive it from her mind. 'Ever *been* to Bridlington, Mat?'

'Oh yes, loads of times. There's this ice-cream, Nottoriani's. Hmmmm!'

'It's not Bridlington we're going to,' put in Grandad, looking at them in his mirror. 'The museum's at a place called Sewerby, *near* Bridlington.'

'*Sewer*by?' Jenna pulled a face. 'Sewerby as in *sewer*? Don't like the sound of that, do you, Mat?'

'Yuuuuk!' Matty shot out her tongue and clutched her throat.

'It's a nice little village,' murmured the old man. 'Your grandma and I spent our honeymoon there.'

'Oh!' Swamped by scalding embarrassment, Jenna floundered. 'I . . . didn't mean, I mean I didn't know . . .' If the seat had been fitted with an ejector mechanism she'd have blasted herself through the roof, just to vanish. Matty stared at her knees, her mouth a mute gape in a scarlet face.

'It's all right,' said the old man quietly. 'You weren't to know, and anyway it was a long, long time ago.' His voice broke momentarily on the second *long*, then steadied. 'Come on girls, it's a trip to the seaside, no long faces now.'

They were bowling at fifty through some lovely spring countryside, but it was a while before the back seat chat resumed.

Twenty

It was just one upstairs room in a museum called Sewerby Hall. THE AMY JOHNSON ROOM. Portraits of Amy and her parents hung above a marble fireplace, and a model of her green and silver Gipsy Moth, 'Jason', dangled from the centre of the ceiling. Jenna gazed up at it.

'Is *that* what she flew to Australia, Grandad?'

The old man nodded. 'That's it, Jenna. Shark-infested seas she flew that over, all the way to Darwin.'

'Wow! Looks like it'd drop to bits in a wind. What's it made of?'

'Canvas, stretched over a framework of wood.'

Jenna chuckled. 'Not the *model*, Grandad, I mean the actual plane.'

'So do I, love. Canvas and wood, with wire braces for strength. All planes were like that at one time.'

'Blooming hummer, Mr Larwood.' Matty shook her head. 'You wouldn't get *me* up in one of them, sharks or no sharks.'

'No, well . . . that's what made Amy special, Matty. She'd the courage to do things that'd scare most people to death, and she wasn't a big strapping lass either. Frail body, heart of a lion.' He smiled. 'Lion*ess*, I suppose I should say.'

The rest of the room was taken up with glass cases crammed with trophies and souvenirs presented to Amy by individuals, cities and clubs all over the world. There were medals, dolls, boomerangs, keys, cups, clocks, compasses and cigarette boxes. There was a lifesize mannequin wearing Amy's flying suit and a chair made from twenty-four varieties of Australian wood. The two girls browsed the room while the old man stood gazing out of the window. When they'd looked at everything he led them to the shop downstairs and bought a slim book about the life of Amy Johnson for Jenna, and a cap with a Yorkshire rose on it for Matty.

'There's a teashop in the grounds,' he said, 'with crisps and Coke and outside tables if anybody fancies it.'

'*I* do,' nodded Jenna. 'How about you, Mat?'

Matty shook her head. 'No, I never go where there's crisps or Coke or outside tables, Jen. Can't stand 'em.' She grinned, slapped her cap on back to front and cried, 'What are we *waiting* for?'

Twenty-One

'I wonder . . .' Matty tipped the can, poured Coke into her glass, 'if like a hundred years from now there'll be a museum somewhere with a Jenna Finch room in it.'

'Oh *yeah*.' Jenna peeled the cellophane off her straw. 'As *if*.'

The old man smiled, stirring his tea. 'Well, you never know. Trouble nowadays is, everything's been done. I mean, planes fly practically everywhere on a daily basis. There are no epic journeys waiting for some intrepid pioneer to attempt. What they do now is, they try going round the world in a hot-air balloon or a plane you have to pedal like a bike, and I just can't see the point in that. No.' He shook his head. 'There *are* still genuine challenges, but they're different. For instance, your brother says there are no women airline captains because nobody'd fly with one. He's wrong of course, there *are* women captains, but there aren't many yet and they're seen as a sort of novelty because there's still this prejudice about women handling complex machinery. In my day it was women drivers, now it's women pilots. The challenge facing you, Jenna, and others like you, is to kill off that prejudice by becoming damn fine pilots so that airlines will have to make you captains whether they want to or not.' He grinned. 'It won't get you your own museum, but it'll mean that by the time you're my age it'll be people like Ned with their outdated prejudices who belong in glass cases.'

They sipped their drinks, gazing out across lawns and flowerbeds. Jenna was thinking about the gun, she couldn't help it. Ned's name had come up and that was that. She looked at her grandad. 'Have you . . . I don't suppose your gun's turned up, Grandad?'

He shook his head. 'No, love, it hasn't and it won't, because somebody's pinched it. I should never have pinched it myself of course, back there in Palestine.'

'You *pinched* it?' She couldn't imagine Grandad stealing.

'Oh yes, I pinched it.' He pulled a face. 'You don't come by firearms honestly, love.' He sipped his tea with a faraway look in his eyes. 'We were searching a house, three of us. Jock Wilkie, Butch Weston and me. Suspected Irgun hideout. There was nobody there so we split up and I went upstairs. There was a cupboard in one of the bedrooms. Big walk-in cupboard with a high shelf. I went up on tiptoe and felt along, carefully in case of booby-traps. There was something heavy, wrapped in cloth. I unwrapped it and it was a revolver.' He shook his head. 'I don't know what came over me. I mean, it was a court-martial offence what I did, but I still did it. It was heavy and glossy and . . . I don't know, *beautiful* in a strange way and I wanted it. I remember thinking *finder's keepers*, sort of thing a kid'll say. Anyway I slipped my pack off and shoved the thing inside. It hardly made a bulge, I knew I could get away with it and I did. "All clear!" I yells down the stairs and I go clattering down, and my mates haven't found anything so we go out and report to the lieutenant. All clear.' He shrugged. 'That was that. I

61

never let on I had it, not even to my best mate. Hid it in my kit till my tour was up, brought it home on disembarkation leave. Loads of fellows did similar things, brought souvenirs back, same in all wars. Guns. Grenades. Daggers. Stupid, but we were only lads, you see. Only lads.'

Jenna nodded. There didn't seem to be anything to say. They finished their drinks, watching people come and go. After a while the old man started to get up. 'There's a little road-train goes down into Brid. We could catch it if you like, have a look at the sea, find some fish and chips for lunch. That sound OK to you?'

It sounded fine. They left the park and walked down to the clifftop road. The wind was stronger here, coming off the sea. The girls zipped up their jackets, waiting for the train.

Twenty-Two

They were back in Haverham at half-eight. They dropped Matty at her door and Jenna transferred herself to the front seat for the short ride to West Lane. She assumed Grandad would come in for a cup of tea but he shook his head. 'Not tonight, love, listen.' He gazed at her. 'I didn't want to mention this in front of your friend, but your brother popped in to see me after school on Tuesday.'

Jenna's heart kicked. 'Y . . . yes, he said he was going to.'

'The thing is, Jenna, I'm pretty certain he's the only person apart from myself who's been in my house since I put that gun away last Sunday, and I was wondering if you'd noticed anything unusual in his behaviour at all.'

'Unusual? I . . . I'm not sure, Grandad. I mean, I don't know what's *usual* in Ned's behaviour. You know what he's like.'

The old man nodded. 'He's a typical teenager, but was he there when you mentioned the gun to your mum and dad?'

'Well yes, but . . .'

'Did he seem interested?'

'Well . . . I think he asked what sort it was, but *anybody*'d be interested wouldn't they? I mean it's not every day you

63

hear about somebody in your family having a gun by their bed.' She looked at him. 'Grandad, are you saying you think *Ned* stole it?' *I can get it back. I* know *I can.*

The old man shook his head. 'I don't want to believe that, Jenna, but I've turned it over and over in my mind and it always comes back to this: the gun was there, then Ned called, then the gun *wasn't* there.' He sighed. 'Do they know it's missing? Your mum and dad, I mean?'

Jenna shook her head. '*I* haven't told them.'

'Why not?'

'Well – I didn't think you'd want people to know. I mean, what you said about crime . . . the police . . .'

'Hmmm!' The old man frowned. 'Or is it that you couldn't tell them because Ned's been showing interest and they might put two and two together?'

'No, it's just . . . Grandad, I think everything'll work out all right without . . . you know, the police and everything. I couldn't stand it if you or . . . or anybody got arrested.' She was close to tears.

'All right, Jenna, it's all right.' He patted her hand. 'We'll leave it for now, but don't you go doing anything silly, d'you hear?' He looked into her eyes. 'If you know something, and I believe you might, you must come to me or your dad because this isn't *Flight Simulator*. In *this* game, dead is dead. A gun is a terrible weapon and if this one doesn't turn up soon, I'm going to have to tell the police and take the consequences.' He leaned across, opened the door for her. 'Tell your mum I was tired from driving and needed an early night. What else you tell her is up to you.' He smiled briefly. 'But only for the moment.'

Twenty-Three

Monday, eight twenty. Two boys behind the science block. Lassiter lights up, draws deeply on the cigarette and exhales, looking at Ned through the smoke. 'So how'd it go?'

'I did like you said, Gav, got it out of my room.'

'Good. Where is it?'

'In a safe place.'

'I said, where?'

'Know the allotments on Moorhouse Lane?'

Lassiter sucks in smoke, shakes his head. 'Digging's not me, Ned.' Ned thinks how cool Gavin looks, the way the smoke curls out of his mouth as he speaks. 'Tell me you didn't leave it where some senile gimmer's gonna trip up over it.'

''Course not, Gav. Half the plots're abandoned, derelict, never been touched in years. There's one with a shed, old pigeon loft, belonged to a guy called Rudyard when I was a kid. He's dead, been dead yonks. I put it there.'

'Oh yeah?' Lassiter taps the cigarette, ash falls on the tarmac. 'And how d'you know some bunch of kids aren't using this shed as a den, you mammal?'

Ned shakes his head. 'They're not, it's too far from where kids live. And anyway it's this high in weeds and if someone'd waded through 'em they'd be trampled.'

'Hmmm. You better show me after school. I don't fancy wasting my time planning this little job, only to find some scruffy Haverham brat's gone off with the hardware.'

'I'm telling you, Gav, it's safe. Why can't you trust me?'

'Listen.' Lassiter drops the cigarette, grinds it under his shoe, locks eyes with Ned. 'Number one, nobody tells me, I tell them. And number two, there's a rule, a golden rule when you're lining up a deal like this: trust nobody, especially not a hick from the sticks like you Finch, so.' He picks up his sport bag, shoulders it. 'Half-three by the bus stop, and that weird sister of yours better not be hanging around or she's gonna find herself in big trouble.' He turns and stalks off, the Adidas bag joggling on his shoulder.

Ned shrugs, picks up his own bag and follows, wishing he'd never let the other boy talk him into those shoplifting expeditions round the mall. He was Lassiter's accomplice, and once you're an accomplice you're in. There's no way out . . .

Twenty-four

Four fifteen. Amy Finch, chopping knife in hand, looked round as her daughter walked in. The crust of bread clamped between her teeth wagged as she spoke. 'Wheryoubinitsaquarterpastfour.'

Jenna laughed, dumping her bag on a chair. 'EyecantearyouMumyougotbredinyermouth.'

'Thascoseyemchoppinonionsyoutwit.' Amy put down the knife, removed the crust. 'I said where have you been, it's a quarter past four.'

'Right. I stayed behind so old Worldwide could show me how to get the best out of *Flight Simulator*.'

'You and your *Flight Simulator*. Did you by any chance see Ned? He's late too.'

Jenna shook her head. 'No, Mum, I didn't. I try to avoid him nowadays 'cause he's always with that slimeball Lassiter.'

'*Slimeball*? Where on earth do you get these horrible expressions from, darling?'

Jenna shrugged. 'TV, I expect, Mum. Anyway slimeball's a compliment when you're talking about Gavin Lassiter. What are we having?'

'Liver and onions, eventually.'

'Oooh yuk!'

'Your dad's favourite.'

'That's 'cause he was dragged up in Bradford.'

'Nonsense, Jenna, liver and onions is a traditional English dish. *And* it's good for you, which is more than can be said for . . . oh by the way, a letter came for you. It's in the front room.'

Jenna carried the long cream envelope up to her room. A crest on the back flap featured a winged shield with the letters HCAA in it. Trying not to get too excited she sat on her bed, slit the envelope with her South Park paperknife and pulled out two folded sheets. One was a dense printout which looked boring. She dropped it on the duvet and smoothed out the letter. It had the crest at the top over the words HAMPSHIRE COLLEGE OF AVIATION AND AERONAUTICS. A shiver went through her as she started to read.

Dear Ms Finch

I refer to your letter dated April 8th and thank you for your enquiry. The college offers a wide range of pilot-training courses, including one for students with no previous flying experience. I have enclosed a full prospectus for your perusal. You may be interested to know that our annual Open Day falls this year on May 16th. If you would care to come along on that occasion my colleagues and myself will be delighted to meet you. If in the meantime you have questions, please don't hesitate to write or fax me at the above address and I will do all I can to assist.

Assuring you of our best attention at all times, I am

Yours sincerely
J. Caverham-Lesney
Chief Flying Instructor

'Yessss!' Jenna leapt up, tossed the letter in the air and ran to the top of the stairs. 'Mum, it's from the Air College and they want to *see* me.' She spread her arms for wings and swooped downstairs thinking, *I bet J. Caverham-Lesney never has liver and onions.*

Twenty-five

Peter Finch skimmed the letter, passed it across the table. 'It's a standard sort of business letter, sweetheart, I wouldn't get too excited.'

'But they want to *meet* me, Dad, it says so.'

'Yes, love, I know, but they'll say that to everybody who enquires. Do they know how young you are?'

'Well no, but they don't ask so maybe it doesn't matter.'

'Hah!' Ned stabbed a bit of liver with his fork. 'What if you were *four*, you turkey? D'you think they'd be dying to meet you then, let you loose in one of their planes?'

'Don't be stupid. If I were four I couldn't have written to them, could I?'

He shrugged. 'Just 'cause you can write doesn't mean you can fly.'

'Eat your dinner, Ned,' growled their father. 'Let me see the prospectus, Jenna.'

'It's upstairs, Dad, I haven't looked at it myself yet. Want me to get it?'

'Yes please.'

She didn't spread her arms for wings but plodded up the stairs, muttering to herself. 'Why do Mum and Dad act like total miseries every time I mention flying? Ned I can understand, he was *born* a donkey, but Mum and Dad, you'd think they'd be . . . you know, a bit supportive. I bet he only wants the prospectus so he can spoil everything.'

'Listen.' Dad read aloud. '*The average age at enrolment is twenty-four years, and most entrants are graduates. The college admits a few students at eighteen if they are exceptionally mature and have a minimum of three A Levels. Applicants over thirty are considered only if they hold a private pilot's licence.*' He lowered the printout, looked at Jenna. 'Eighteen, sweetheart, *if* you're exceptionally mature and have three A Levels.'

'Huh!' sneered Ned, 'she's about as mature as a newborn baby.'

His father eyeballed him. 'A mature brother isn't forever baiting his younger sister, so I suggest you shut up, eat up and grow up.' Ned blushed and stared at his plate. Peter Finch turned to his daughter. 'I really think you'll be wasting your time if you go to this Open Day, Jenna. J. Caverham-Lesney obviously assumes you're far older than you are. Why not put the college address on computer and get in touch in, say, three years' time?'

Jenna stared at the tablecloth. An hour ago she'd been happy, filled with optimism. She wanted to cling to at least a shred of that feeling. 'I could go, Dad, couldn't I, just look round, talk to somebody?' *Say yes. Say you'll take me.*

Her father shrugged. 'You could, I suppose, but then there's the cost to consider.'

'The cost?' How much could it cost to go to Hampshire, for goodness' sake? 'Hampshire's not far, Dad, it wouldn't cost that much.'

He chuckled, shaking his head. 'Not *that* cost,

sweetheart. I'm not talking about the cost of going to Hampshire, I mean the cost of going to this college. Have you *looked* at these fees?'

'No, I told you, I didn't check out the prospectus. How much is it?'

'Commercial pilot's course, starting from scratch, about thirty thousand pounds.' He looked at her. 'I'm sorry, sweetheart, that sort of dosh is totally out of our reach, and barring a win on the Lottery it'll be just as far beyond us when you're eighteen. I'm afraid if you're going to be a pilot you'll have to find another way of getting there.'

'Thanks, Dad, thanks a lot.' Jenna threw down her napkin, shoved back her chair and stood up. 'I *knew* this'd happen as soon as you mentioned the prospectus. I knew you just wanted to spoil everything, you always *do*.' Tears blurred her vision, spilling onto her cheeks. 'I feel like killing myself,' she choked, 'and if I do it'll be all your fault.'

'Jenna!' Her mother rose and reached for her, but Jenna whirled and ran from the room. *Just you wait*, she thought, stumbling up the stairs. *See how you like it with me dead and your precious Ned in a cell with Grandad and our pictures splashed all over the front page of the* Target. *You won't feel like sitting there stuffing yourselves with liver and onions then, spoiling people's lives.* She slammed her door and threw herself across the bed.

Twenty-Six

Nine o'clock. Albert Larwood sleeps in the armchair and this is his dream.

It is 1936 and he's thirteen, in the scullery of his mother's house on Rose Street. She takes in washing and the place is full of steam. Albert should be at school, but there's only one pair of boots and it's Ernest's turn to wear them. Some mothers send their children barefoot but not Sarah Larwood.

'Mam?'

'What is it, Bertie?' She claws wet hair from her brow with a raw hand.

'Billy Lee's dad says there'll be a war soon.'

'It'd be better if Billy Lee's dad did a bit less talking and a bit more looking for work.'

'Yes, Mam, but if there is a war, d'you think they'd let me be a pilot?'

'Nay, lad.' His mother leans her wooden tongs against the rim of the copper and straightens up, wincing at the ache in her back. 'Don't you think this family's had enough of fighting? Both your grandads died in the Great War and before that I lost an uncle in South Africa. I hope there's never another war,

73

but if there is I want you and your brother in nice safe jobs, not up in the sky being shot at.'

'I know, Mam, but flying's the only thing I want to do and I just thought a war might give me a chance.' He sighs. 'Amy Johnson broke the record to South Africa the other day.'

'You and your Amy Johnson.' His mother nods towards the mangle. 'Turn this for me will you, our Bertie?' She begins feeding a shirt into the rollers. 'Amy Johnson went to a posh school. She'd her own shoes so she could go regularly, and she had a dad. Her mam didn't have to take in washing, and she wasn't waiting for Amy to turn fourteen and go to work in the mill and bring in a few shillings.' She catches the flattened shirt, throws it on the pile, reaches for another. 'People like us aren't wanted for pilots, Bertie, even in wartime. There's plenty of posh, clever lads'll fly their planes for them while you and our Ernest get sent to the trenches to be blown to bits or drowned in a flipping shell-hole. No.' She shakes her head. 'We want no wars, and the sooner you stop mooning over Miss Amy Johnson and make your mind up you'll be starting at Longlands Mill in a few months' time, the better.'

The old man wakes, his mother's voice lingering. 'Mam?' he murmurs, turning his head a little, seeing first the hand of an old man on the chair-arm, then the framed snapshot of his wife on the sideboard. Gone, both of them, where only dreams can reach. A tear forms at the corner of his eye and follows the course of a wrinkle down the side of his face.

Twenty-Seven

Tuesday breakfast was awful. Mum shoved the cornflakes at her, then chatted with Dad as if Jenna wasn't even there. She knew what they were waiting for. They were waiting for her to say sorry, but she couldn't. She didn't *feel* sorry. Well – perhaps she did a bit, but not enough to say it. Ned smirked every time he caught her eye, so she avoided looking at him. She'd have liked more milk on her cornflakes but wouldn't ask anybody to pass the jug.

It isn't fair. Here's me, trying to sort this gun thing without Grandad getting in trouble; without Ned getting into trouble even, and what do I get? Ignored, that's what. Smirked at. Told I can't be a pilot. I know it's sort of my fault for mentioning the thing in the first place but still, if it wasn't for Grandad I'd tell, this minute, see Ned laugh on the other side of his face.

Breakfast dragged. It felt like for ever before Dad got up and went to reverse the car out and Mum started clearing the table. Nobody had said a single word to Jenna. She waited till Mum was at the sink with her back to them, then leaned towards her brother and murmured, 'You pinched Grandad's gun. He knows it and so do I.'

75

'Oh yeah?' Ned smirked. 'Prove it. Search my room. Call the police if you like.'

Jenna shook her head. 'No police, Grandad'd go to jail. Take it back Ned, *please*. I'll never tell anyone.'

'You're wasting your breath, Sis. The gun's not here, and even if it was I wouldn't give it up for *you*, you're so pathetic.' He got up and walked out of the room.

Pathetic. Jenna stared at her mother's reproachful back, clean out of ideas. *Search my room*. Yes, she could do that but she wouldn't find anything. If the gun was there he wouldn't have invited her to search, which meant he had it somewhere else, or maybe he'd passed it on to somebody. *Only for the moment*, Grandad had said. She'd told the old man everything would work out but he wasn't going to wait for ever. *I need to talk to somebody*, she thought, *but who? Who can I talk to about a thing like this who won't go running to the police or a teacher or Mum and Dad or somebody?*

Matty.

Twenty-Eight

'Hey, Mat.' Lunchtime. The two girls at the sandwich table, eating grub from home.

'What?'

'Gotta talk to you, something important.'

'So what you waiting for – an appointment?'

'No, listen, this is serious. You know the other Friday at my grandad's, all that stuff about the gun?'

'Sure I remember. You promised to explain, then didn't. A family thing, I think you said.'

Jenna nodded. 'That's right I did, and it's still a family thing only I need you to be a sort of honorary Finch for a bit 'cause I'll go bananas if I can't share this with someone.'

'Ah.' Matty reached for the water-jug, poured herself a glass. 'Water?'

'No thanks.'

Matty sipped, gazed at her friend over the rim of the glass. 'Go on then.'

Jemma pulled a face. 'This isn't easy, Mat. You see, I know who pinched the gun.'

'You *do*?' Matty nearly choked. 'Who?'

'Sssh!' Jenna glanced around at the other sandwich

eaters. Nobody seemed interested. 'Not so loud. It's my brother.'

'Ned?'

'I only have the one brother, Mat.'

'How d'you know he's got it – have you *seen* it?'

'No I haven't, but I can tell by the way he acts.'

'And what does he want it for, Jen?'

Jenna shook her head. 'That's the six million dollar question isn't it? I don't believe he means to do anything really bad, Mat, but I wish he hadn't got it and I don't know what I can do without getting people in trouble. I mean, people go to the police with stuff like this but if I do that Grandad'll be in bother for having the gun in the first place and Ned'll be arrested and it'll get into the papers and you know what my mum's like about the neighbours and all that.'

Matty nodded. 'He probably just wants to show off with it, Jen. You know what boys're like. Have you tried talking to him?'

''Course I have. First thing I thought of.'

'And?'

Jenna shrugged. 'And nothing. Says he hasn't got it, I can search his room. Which means it's not in his room of course.'

'So where'd you think it is, Jen?'

'I haven't a clue.' Jenna looked at her friend. 'What the heck can I *do*, Mat?'

'Well.' Matty snapped the lid on her sandwich box, crammed it in her pack. 'Only thing I can think of is, find out where he's hidden it and pinch it back.'

'Yeah but like, how? How'm I supposed to find out where he's hidden it – *ask* him?'

'*Follow* him, Jen. If a lad's got a gun I bet he can't resist gawping at it now and then, holding it in his hand, pretending he's Eddie Murphy or Harvey Keitel or one of that lot. Follow him, Jen, everywhere. He'll lead you to the gun if he's got it. I'll help you if you like.'

'You *will*?'

''Course.' Matty grinned. 'It could be a laugh. Why don't we start today, after school?'

Twenty-Nine

Worldwide intercepted her in the corridor at the start of afternoon break. 'Any better on the simulator nowadays, Jenna?'

'Oh yes sir, thanks.' She'd hardly touched the simulator for days, too much on her mind, but she couldn't tell Mr Webb that.

'Found the challenges have you, flying under bridges and so on?'

'Yes sir. I tried the Eiffel Tower but couldn't get under. Kept hitting the ground.'

The teacher nodded. 'Not surprised. I remember that one, it's tough. Did that college respond by the way: the one you were writing to?'

Jenna pulled a face. 'Yes sir, they invited me to their Open Day next month but I don't think I'll be going. My dad read the letter, found out it's thirty K to learn, more or less told me to forget it.'

'Oh, but you *mustn't*.' Worldwide shook his head. 'I found some stuff on the net and yes, pilot training *is* expensive, but trainees don't usually pay the full whack themselves, Jenna. You can be sponsored by an airline which will employ you once you're qualified and deduct the fees from your salary till you're quits.'

'Is that right sir, *really*?' She felt her heart lift.

'Yes it's right, *really*. I'll download it again if you like, print it off so you can show your dad.' He grinned. 'You never know: you might find yourself boogying on down to that Open Day yet, young Jenna.' He strode off towards the staffroom. Jenna gazed after him, then ran outside to share her good news with Matty.

Thirty

It was easy. The school was on one side of Butt Lane and the park was on the other. All the two girls had to do at half-three was cross the lane and hop over the park wall. It was only a metre high so they squatted down among the rhododendrons and peeped over, watching the school gate. Jenna hoped Ned wouldn't have Gavin Lassiter with him, and for once he didn't. He came out alone and strode off up Butt Lane, his Adidas bag bouncing on his shoulder. The girls followed at a crouching run on their side of the wall to the top of the lane, where Ned and a bunch of other pupils crossed Rawdon Road with the help of the lollipop lady.

'I think he's just going home,' said Jenna as she and Matty left the park.

Matty shook her head. 'You don't know yet.' They had to wait till another knot of kids accumulated at the crossing and the attendant stopped the traffic for them. By the time they got to the bottom of Main Street Ned was halfway up. 'He *is* going home,' muttered Jenna. 'No point you going past your place, Mat.'

'I'll come as far as Church Street,' insisted Matty. 'You never know – he might be heading for Penistone Hill.'

Jenna shrugged. 'Doubt it, but come if you want. There's something I want to show you anyway.'

They tailed Ned as he crossed the museum car park on to West Lane. By this time it was obvious Jenna was right: he was heading home.

'Never mind,' smiled Matty, 'couldn't really expect anything thrilling to happen the first time. There's always tomorrow.'

'Yeah but like, I don't have endless time, Mat.'

'I know that, Jen, but we can't *force* him to lead us to the gun. All we can do is keep trying. You said you wanted to show me something.'

'Yeah, it's nothing much, you might have seen it. Over here.' She led her friend to the aeroplane stone and pointed. Matty gazed down at the engraved slab. 'No, I've never seen this. When did you do it?'

Jenna laughed. 'I didn't do it, my grandad did.'

'Your grandad Larwood, the one who . . .?'

Jenna nodded. 'He did it when he was a kid, but I didn't know that till the other day. I've passed it every schoolday since I was five and I never knew he did it.' She smiled. 'I used to think it was magic.'

'Magic – why?'

'Well, it had my mum's name on it for a start. Amy. I'd never heard of Amy Johnson then of course. Couldn't understand how a flagstone came to have my mum's name on it. I wouldn't step on it in case I made something awful happen to her, and I kept it clean of leaves and twigs and stuff. Dog-dirt, even. To be perfectly honest I still do.'

Matty chuckled. 'So you still think it's magic?'

'In a way I suppose I do, especially since I found out Grandad carved it. I mean it's weird isn't it, the way I looked after it all those years even though I didn't realize there was like a family connection?'

Matty nodded. 'I suppose so, yes.' She grinned. 'Hey – maybe you should ask the stone to help you sort this gun thing.'

Jenna shook her head. 'You're laughing, aren't you? I shouldn't have shown it to you.'

'I'm not laughing, Jen. Try it, I mean it. It might not do any good but it can't do any harm.'

'All right then.' Jenna cleared her throat, fixed her gaze on the flag. 'Aeroplane stone,' she intoned, 'as the granddaughter of your maker, I ask you to lend some of your magic power in a good cause.'

'Amen,' murmured Matty. The two girls looked at each other for a second, then burst out laughing.

'I can't believe we *did* that,' spluttered Jenna. 'What are we, three years old or something?'

'At the most,' gasped Matty. 'I'd better go before we start singing Toby Tall. See you.' She walked off shaking her head.

Jenna watched her out of sight, then looked down once more at the stone. 'I believe,' she whispered. Then she turned for home.

Thirty-One

'Dad?' Six o'clock. The Finch family round the table, eating dinner. Lamb chops, butter beans, mashed potato. They seemed to have stopped ignoring her so Jenna had decided to push her luck.

'What is it, Jenna?'

Oh-ho, so it's Jenna, not sweetheart. Leave it a bit. 'Nothing, Dad.'

'Oh come on, it must be *something*. Spit it out.'

She noticed Ned looking across at her, his fork halfway to his mouth. Nervous then. She was glad.

'It's just ... you know the thirty K the college wants to train a pilot?'

'Ye-es?'

'Well the thing is, Dad, you don't have to find it yourself.'

'Oh now *that*'s a relief.' Sarcasm time. 'Load off my mind, that is. So who *does* find it, Jenna, your fairy godmother?'

'No, an airline. You pay it back bit by bit when you start working for them. Mr Webb told me.'

'Did he now?' Her father speared three beans with his fork. 'And did Mr Webb also explain what happens when a trainee fails the course and never gets to be a pilot? How does the thirty K get repaid *then*?'

'I . . . no, he didn't mention that but it's one of the things I could ask, isn't it, at the Open Day?'

Peter Finch sighed and put down his fork. 'Listen, sweetheart, there isn't going to *be* any Open Day. For you I mean, and I'll tell you why. You're thirteen. You've another five years of school, then hopefully university. That's eight years. Eight years before you'll be in a position to start applying for jobs. You'll be twenty-one, and if you're like most youngsters you'll have changed your mind about what you want to do not once, but half a dozen times.' He gazed at her. 'Do you know what I wanted to be when I was thirteen?'

Jenna stared at the tablecloth. 'What?'

'A deep sea diver.' He snorted. 'Can you see it, *me*, groping about in the dark under some ruddy great oilrig, looking for leaks or cracks or whatever it is they do? I can't think of anything nastier, but you see at thirteen I hadn't a clue what deep sea divers are actually *for*. I pictured myself wandering about on a coral reef, looking out through my face-plate at shoals of tropical fish in warm, crystal water. I didn't actually have anything to *do* down there, unless it was collecting pearls or sponges or pirate gold. I'd no idea what deep sea diving actually entailed, only that it sounded exciting and glamorous and *different*, and that's how you see flying planes, Jenna.' He picked up his fork. 'When you've done it for a bit, flying an airliner's probably like driving a bus only not as interesting because there's nothing to look at, but your mum and I have been talking and I'll tell you what.' He gazed at her. 'Give it two years. If you're still keen at sixteen we'll find a way to get you some flying lessons. All right?'

'Two years?' *Flipping long time. A lifetime. Still it's positive, which makes a change.* She smiled, nodded. 'Yeah, thanks Dad, that's fair.' *He thinks I'll go off it in the meantime but I won't.* She speared a bean. *He's promised now, and you can bet I'll hold him to it.*

Thirty-Two

Ned slips into the pigeon loft at dusk. Lassiter is sitting on a ledge in the semi-darkness, smoking. 'Ten past eight,' he grunts, 'you're late.'

'Only ten minutes,' Ned protests. 'Couldn't get away. Listen.' He joins his friend on the ledge. 'How soon's this thing coming off, Gav?'

'Why?'

'It's my sister. She reckons she knows I took the gun. She could grass me up to Mum and Dad anytime. I keep expecting her to and it's doing my head in.'

'I'm asking myself two things,' drawls Lassiter, mashing the stub of his cigarette on the ledge. 'One, why do you think it's OK to show up late when my plan calls for split-second timing, and two, if you're gonna let a little girl do your head in, what'll you be like when you have to face a couple of trained security guards?'

'It's not the same, Gav. I'll be on time when it matters, and the security guard thing'll be over in seconds, not dragging on day after day like this thing with Jenna.'

'Well, I dunno.' Lassiter plucks a fresh cigarette from his pack, places it between his lips, lights it with the old Zippo

88

whose clunk is so much a part of his cool image. 'See, on a job like this a guy needs a dependable partner and I'm thinking maybe you're not it, Finch. I'm thinking maybe I should be looking elsewhere, know what I'm saying?'

Ned sees his chance, shrugs. Mustn't seem too eager. 'Well if that's how you feel, Gav, maybe . . .'

'Ha!' The other boy sneers. 'You'd like that wouldn't you, Ned, off the hook, but it's not that easy. I mean, you know too much. It wouldn't just be a matter of dropping you and getting a replacement. I'd have to silence you.'

'H-how d'you mean, silence?'

'Oh, I think you know what I mean.' Lassiter sticks out two fingers, holds them to Ned's temple. 'There's only one way to silence somebody. One sure way.'

Ned swallows. 'You wouldn't.'

'I would, you know I would, but no: I'm not going to drop you, Ned. It's you and me all the way.' He looks sidelong at his miserable accomplice. 'How fond are you of that sister of yours?'

'What d'you mean?'

'It's a simple question, Finch. How fond of her are you? What would you be prepared to do to get her off your back?'

'Well . . .' Ned flounders. 'I wouldn't . . . you know, hurt her. Beat her up or anything like that.'

'You wouldn't?' Lassiter takes the cigarette out of his mouth, examines its glowing tip. 'I would, no danger, especially if she was jeopardising my operation.' He glances at the other boy. 'Are you soft, Finch?'

'N . . . not soft enough to let you hurt Jenna, Gav, not even for the operation. In fact, if you even hint at anything like that again I'll take the gun and own up and that'll be the end of it.'

'End of it?' Lassiter chuckles nastily. 'Oh no, Finch, that won't be the end of it, more like the beginning.' He leans forward, gazes into Ned's eyes. 'Tell me Finch, d'you read the papers?'

Ned moistens his lips with his tongue, shrugs. 'We get the Telegraph *and the local rag, the* Target.'

Lassiter shakes his head. 'Probably didn't make the Target but it was in the Telegraph *and on TV. Two brothers, fifteen and twelve, rushed to hospital on different nights minus their thumbs. Town in the Midlands. Awful thing. Neither kid could describe his assailant so they never caught anybody.' He laughs. 'Thumbs Down, headline in one tabloid. Talk about bad taste.'*

Lassiter's smoke has filled the loft. Ned clears his throat. 'I think I remember it. What's it got to do with. . .?'

Lassiter looks at him, wide-eyed. 'Oh nothing, nothing at all. No, it popped into my head that's all. D'you know it's our thumbs that separate us from the animals, Finch?'

'H . . . how d'you mean?'

'Humans. We humans have what they call opposed thumbs. They flex the opposite way to our fingers, means we can grip things. Tools. Our ancestors could use tools, make things. Nothing else could. That's how we came to dominate. Why our brains developed, except here in Haverham I mean. It's stuffed you'd be without your thumbs old son, totally stuffed.' He sighs. 'Two quick chops and you might as well have been born a monkey. Anyway,' he smiles, 'that's not what we're here to talk about, is it, so let's get on. I've been observing, timing things, and what it boils down to is . . .'

Thirty-Three

While her brother sat with his tormentor in Rudyard's pigeon loft, Jenna lay on her bed reading the Amy Johnson book Grandad had bought her at Sewerby. She read how Amy's parents wanted her to be a secretary, and how she tried it but couldn't settle so she wrote to the de Havilland flying school to ask about lessons but found it was too expensive. 'Tell me about it,' muttered Jenna. 'Five quid an hour – wish it was that *now*.' She read on and learned that Amy eventually got lessons for one pound fifty by joining an aeroplane club, but after her first lesson her instructor told her she was no good: she'd never make a pilot.

No good! Jenna thought about the Amy Johnson Room at Sewerby. All those trophies. *She probably ended up twice as good as that instructor, but what if she'd taken notice of him and given up? She'd have ended up as a secretary, wouldn't she? An unhappy secretary nobody'd ever hear of. Her mum and dad might have been happy but it wasn't their life, it was hers, just like mine's mine.*

Mine's mine. She picked up her mobile, punched in Grandad's number and waited. It always took him a while to get to the phone.

'Grandad.'

'Oh, hello Jenna. How are things?'

'Not bad. I've been reading the book you bought me.'

'Book?'

'Yeah, you know – Amy Johnson?'

'Oh, *that* book. Some girl, wasn't she?'

'Yes. I . . . I hope this isn't cheeky, Grandad, but I'm wondering if you'd drive me somewhere again.'

'Back to Sewerby?'

'No, Grandad, a bit further. Hampshire.'

'Hampshire! I'll *say* it's a bit further. About as far as I've ever been in fact.'

'What about Palestine?'

The old man chuckled. 'I didn't have to *drive* to Palestine, young woman, and besides I was young and fit, not like now. Anyway, what's Hampshire got that we haven't?'

'It's got the Hampshire College of Aviation and Aeronautics.'

'Has it indeed? And what's the connection between the Hampshire College of Aviation and whatsit, and a certain Miss Jenna Finch?'

'I got a letter from 'em. Hang on and I'll read it to you.'

'I see,' said her grandad when she'd read out the letter. 'And what about your mum and dad – can't *they* take you to this Open Day?'

Jenna sighed. 'They could but they *won't*, Grandad. They say I'm to wait till I'm sixteen, and besides Dad says it costs too much.'

'Ah.' There was a brief silence. 'As a matter of interest Jenna, how much *does* it cost?'

'The full thing? Thirty thousand pounds.'

'Huh – and here *I* was thinking it might be expensive.'

'*What*?'

The old man laughed. 'Joke, lovey. Your dad's absolutely right, you know. That sort of money's way beyond the reach of folk like you and me. D'you think there'd be any *point* going to this Open Day, even if I took you against your parents' wishes, which I wouldn't?'

'I think so, yes.' Jenna explained how airlines sometimes sponsored students. 'I'd pay them back you see, out of my captain's pay, but if you won't take me anyway . . .'

'Hey, not so glum, sweetheart, eh? Amy couldn't afford it either but *she* didn't give up.' He chuckled. 'Listen, I wasn't going to tell you this, it was going to be a surprise but never mind. It's your birthday the first of next month, isn't it?'

Jenna frowned. 'Ye-es.'

'Fourteen, right?'

'Yes, but . . .?'

'OK, listen. I've got your birthday present here in the sideboard drawer. Know what it is?'

'No, Grandad, how could I?'

'Then I'll tell you. It's a voucher.'

'A voucher . . . what sort of voucher?'

'The sort of voucher that'll get you a trial flying lesson at an aeroplane club not far from here. May first's a Sunday, so it's very convenient.'

'A . . . *flying* lesson?' It came out squeaky. 'You mean a *real* one, in a *plane*?'

Her grandad laughed. 'Well I *hope* it'll be in a plane, sweetheart. If it turns out to be in a tractor I'll want my money back.'

'But . . . *wow*, Grandad, I don't know what to say. I'll try really *really* hard, you'll see. He won't say *I'm* no good like he did Amy . . .'

'I doubt it'll be the same instructor, sweetheart, and the

idea is that you *enjoy* the experience, not bust a gut trying to outfly poor Amy.'

'Oh I will, Grandad. I *will* enjoy it, thank you, thank you, thank you.'

'Don't mention it.'

'Oh I'll *mention* it all right.' To her surprise she found herself in tears. 'I'll mention it at the top of my voice to everyone in Haverham. Everyone in the *world*. I *love* you, Grandad . . .'

Thirty-four

'Mum, where's Dad?'

Her mother was watching The History Zone. She put it on mute and looked at her daughter. 'Your dad's gone to the pub for an hour, where's the fire?'

'Fire?'

'You're all het up, what's *wrong*?'

'Nothing's *wrong*, Mum, everything's right. Guess what Grandad's got me for my birthday?'

Her mother pulled a face. 'I give up. Must be something pretty good though.' She peered at Jenna. 'Have you been crying?'

'A bit, yeah. He's got me a *flying* lesson, Mum. A *real* one, not a simulator.'

'Oh, Jenna!' Amy Finch aimed the remote, switched off. 'That's wonderful, darling, but your grandad's a pensioner, he can't . . . it must've cost a small fortune. Dad and I'll have to give him the money or at least *share*.'

Jenna shook her head. 'I wouldn't, Mum. It probably *was* expensive but I think he's done it 'cause he wanted to. It's *his* present, it might be spoilt if you . . .'

Her mother nodded. 'I know what you mean, love, and

you're probably right.' She gazed at Jenna. 'Darling, I hope you don't think your dad and I are being deliberately obstructive over this ambition of yours. We're *not*. It's just that what you want is so tremendously expensive and you're still so young and we *do* believe you'll change your mind in a year or . . .'

'I won't.'

'But you can't possibly *know* that, Jenna, not at thirteen.'

'Nearly fourteen, Mum, and I *do* know.' She smiled. 'It's fate, you see. Destiny.'

'Destiny? How d'you make that out?'

'It's obvious. The aeroplane stone. I take care of it, it takes care of me.'

'Nonsense, darling, it's just a flagstone.'

'With a plane on it carved by my grandad, *and* he put his daughter's name on it long before he even knew he'd *have* a daughter, and *something* made me look after it for years and years without knowing Grandad carved it, and this afternoon I asked it to help me and a few hours later here comes my first flying lesson.' She laughed. 'See? Magic.'

Her mother nodded. 'It must seem magical to you, darling. Come here.' She held out her arms and Jenna came into them, kneeling on the rug as she had when she was very young. Her mother spoke softly, stroking her hair and rocking her. 'I'm so, *so* happy for you darling, and I know Daddy will be too. I wish you joy of your flying lesson and I hope it'll turn out to be the first of many, though I can't see how we'll ever manage that.' She smiled. 'And it *is* a kind of magic, you know: the kind where you find happiness because you've made someone else happy.' She sighed. 'I'd begun to think your grandad was slipping away, but you've brought him back with your dreams and your schemes and your old Amy Johnson and *that's* magic, stone or no stone.'

Thirty-Five

She'd gone up to get ready for bed, leaving Mum to tell Dad the news when he came in, when somebody knocked on her door. 'Who is it?'

'Me.' Ned's voice.

Jenna sighed. 'Just a minute.' She threw a towel round her shoulders, opened the door. 'What?' Some sort of hassle. Had to be, knowing Ned, but never mind. Tonight she could handle it.

'Let me in, Sis, it's important.' He looked ill.

'OK.' She stepped aside.

'Thanks. Better shut the door.'

She closed it and faced him. 'What's important, Ned?'

He shook his head. 'You're not going to like it, Sis, but I've got to warn you.'

'*Warn* me?' Jenna frowned. 'What about?'

'About . . . interfering.'

'Interfering?' She snorted. 'It's about the gun isn't it, and *you're* warning *me*? It's *you* that needs warning, you dumbo, letting that veg Lassiter get you into whatever it is. All you have to do is . . .'

'It's not that easy, Jenna. Gav knows you're pressuring

97

me, he's arsed off and he's not a veg, he's dangerous. Crazy even. You've got to stop. I'm *asking* you to lay off.'

Jenna gazed at her brother. 'He's got you scared, hasn't he? Why don't you just . . ?'

'I'm scared for *you*, you spud-head. He mentioned you and then he mentioned something else, something I can't tell you about, but I've got to ask you to back off before he gets on your case. For your own good, Sis, leave it. Read your Amy Johnson book, play *Flight Simulator*, whatever, only stay out of this.' He opened the door, repeated 'Stay out of it,' and headed for his own room.

Thirty-Six

'We doing our Miss Marple bit, Jen?' Wednesday hometime. Matty washing her hands in one of the cloakroom basins. Girls milling, shoving, shouting.

Jenna had been wondering the same thing all day. Whether to drop it in the light of Ned's warning, think of some other way to locate the gun, or risk it, hoping that creep Lassiter wouldn't catch her at it. She'd just about resolved to take a chance, but saw no reason to put her friend in danger. She could still feel the warm glow Matty's hug had given her this morning in the middle of Main Street when she told her about the flying lesson.

'I think *I* will, Mat, but there's no need for you to.' She smiled. 'In fact, one's less likely to be spotted than two.'

'Huh!' Matty ripped a paper towel from the dispenser, rubbed her hands dry. 'I can take a hint y'know, Jen. No time for me I suppose, now you're a trainee flipping pilot.'

Jenna shook her head. 'It's not *that*, Mat. I just don't want to waste your time like yesterday. He'll probably go straight home again.'

Matty screwed up the towel, lobbed it in the bin. 'Well as it happens I'm supposed to pick up Mum's bread order, so I won't stay just this once.' She scowled. *'Just this once*, mind. I'll be back on the job tomorrow whether you want me or not.'

Jenna nodded. 'Fair enough, Mat.' Tomorrow was soon enough to think about tomorrow. 'See you in the morning.' She left the building and hurried across the yard looking for Ned. There was no sign of him, but as she came out onto Butt Lane she saw him halfway up. He was by himself again. She crossed over, keeping an eye open for Gavin Lassiter. There was no sign of him either. She scrambled over the wall and ran crouching through the rhododendrons till she was almost level with her brother, who was walking rapidly with his head down.

She followed till he joined the throng waiting to cross Rawdon Road, then straightened up and was about to throw a leg over the wall when a strong arm encircled her waist, a hand covered her mouth and she was dragged, kicking and spluttering, backwards into a giant rhododendron. The shrub's unpruned branches had spread and drooped till they touched the soil all round, leaving at its heart a dim, dome-shaped space carpeted with dead leaves and concealed by the plant's evergreen foliage. In this natural shelter Jenna was forced into a sitting position on the damp leafmould.

Without relaxing his hold her assailant murmured in her ear, 'Me Tarzan, you Jane, this, jungle: nobody come, nobody see. Now Tarzan show Jane what happen when Jane stick nose in Tarzan business.'

Thirty-Seven

'Matty!'

She looks up in the shop doorway, sees Ned coming down towards her. Transferring her carrier bag to the other hand she waits, the fragrance of newbaked bread in her nostrils.

'Have you seen Jenna, Matty?' He seems anxious, shifting his weight from foot to foot.

Matty shakes her head. 'Saw her in the cloakroom, not since. She left before me.'

'Oh.' He chews his lip. 'I thought you always walked up together.'

'We usually do. I was delayed a bit.'

'Ah. She didn't mention going anywhere, I suppose?'

'Not that I remember.' Where's she got to? 'Was she supposed to meet you or something?'

'No, I just thought I'd see her at the top. I usually do.' He shrugs. 'Doesn't matter.' It did though, Matty could tell. 'See you.' He turns and starts back up.

Matty doesn't know what to do. Jenna was supposed to have been tailing her brother, but if she was he'd have bumped into her when he turned back. Why did he turn back? He's never bothered about Jenna before that I know of. She stands for a minute then sets off downhill, the bread bumping her leg as she walks.

Thirty-Eight

Albert Larwood finishes thinning the row of lettuces, straightens up slowly with a soft groan, hands in the small of his back. It's well after four, getting a bit chilly. He stands gazing west across the picket fence to where a watery sun slides down the sky. He'll pack it in now, make his way home for a pot of tea.

He's turning when a movement catches his eye. Somebody's wading through the waist-high weeds in what used to be Rudyard's patch. Albert moves a bit to his left so he'll be hidden by his shed from whoever's approaching. He's noticed that lately something or somebody has trampled a swathe through the brittle stems of last year's rosebay willow herb round the rickety pigeon loft. He's blamed stray dogs, but it isn't a dog that comes in sight now. It's a youth.

Vandal, murmurs the old man to himself. They've had vandal trouble in the past, these allotments. He wishes he dare show himself, call out, but you hear such frightening tales these days. Albert enjoys his garden, but isn't prepared to be kicked to death defending it. It's only as the lad yanks open the loft door that he recognizes his grandson.

What the heck's Ned doing in a derelict pigeon loft a mile

*away from home? Albert is about to hail the boy when
something stops him. A thought. Suppose his suspicion
regarding Ned – a suspicion he's ashamed of – is true after all?
Suppose it was his grandson who stole the revolver. He'd have
to hide it, wouldn't he, and it'd be highly dodgy to keep it at
home. What if . . . ?*

*He sees that Ned isn't staying. The lad has merely stuck his
head round the door. Now he backs out, pulls the door closed
and retraces his route through the tangle.*

*The old man forces himself to wait a minute or two to let
him get well away, then sets out to investigate the loft for
himself.*

Thirty-Nine

The hand clamped over her mouth hurt. Jenna clawed at it. Fear mounted as she recalled the numerous warnings of parents and teachers about *funny men* in parks and other lonely spots. Funny men, nothing funny about the things they sometimes did. She grabbed the wrist and tugged, but that only hurt her more. As she struggled it dawned on her who this *Tarzan* probably was and a saying crossed her mind. *Better the devil you know.* She felt a bit less terrified, but only a bit.

'Tarzan restyle Jane hair.' He was disguising his voice.

'I know it's you, Lassiter,' she shouted into his palm, but all that emerged was a mumble.

Half heard, half felt a thin crunching, familiar. Something brushed her cheek and tumbled across the back of her hand. A thick comma of fair hair. *He's cutting my hair off.* She let go of his wrist to flail, trying with both hands to knock the scissors away. *He has scissors, must've planned this.*

Her attacker laughed softly. 'Jane not let Tarzan cut hair, Tarzan cut something else. Ears, maybe.'

'No!' She shook her head against the pressure of the clamp, heard the faint grind of steel on steel, froze as blades nipped the tip of her right ear.

'Jane clasp hands in lap, sit very still.'

Having no choice, Jenna subsided. The hand stayed tight across her mouth. The scissors were withdrawn from her ear. She felt him using their point to tease out a second lock. She sobbed, watching herself walk into her mother's kitchen in half an hour's time completely bald.

'Jen?'

Jenna felt her assailant tense at the sound of Matty's voice. She tried to cry out but was gagged as effectively as before.

He put his lips to her ear, showed her the scissors. 'Ssssh! One sound, Jane's eye out.' She didn't doubt it.

'Jen, are you there? Are you all right?' Matty was just the other side of the wall. Jenna could see a bit of her face through the rhododendron, didn't know whether she'd rather her friend went away or persisted. She couldn't see Lassiter but knew from his muted breathing he was watching Matty too.

'Jen? Jenna?' She was leaning over the wall, peering into the shrubbery. Jenna knew she'd be thinking about funny men. There was a scrabbling sound. The bit of face jerked up out of sight. Matty was coming over.

Jenna's attacker yanked her head back and hissed, 'Tarzan go. Jane turn round, Tarzan hurt Jane friend. Pull teefs out, maybe.'

As Matty's clumpy shoes hit the soil, Jenna's mouth was freed. She inhaled deeply but didn't turn round. When thin hands parted the foliage and Matty peered in there was only her friend, sitting in the leafmould looking pale, with a lock of hair in her lap.

105

Forty

The old man leaves the door open for light and pokes around but the place is bare. Whatever equipment a pigeon loft usually contains is long gone. A narrow shelf runs the length of one wall and there are some cigarette ends on the floor, which means somebody's been using the place apart from Ned because he doesn't smoke. Albert sits on the shelf, thinking about Rudyard. He and Rudyard occupied adjoining allotments for more than twenty years and never spoke to each other beyond a mumbled 'morning now and then. Not a chatty bloke, old Rudyard. Albert would see him pottering around the loft, removing waste and carrying in feed and water, talking softly all the time to his birds. In World War Two the young Rudyard had been captured at Dunkirk and had spent the rest of the war in prison camps. Halfway through the war he'd got a letter from his wife to say she'd fallen for somebody else, and local gossip reckoned that's what turned him strange. Didn't care for women after that. Or men. Loved his pigeons though. Liked to set them free, watch them fly away. Perhaps it reminded him of the day in 1945 when an American tank flattened the camp gate and set him free.

Thinking about Rudyard's wife reminds Albert of his own, as most things do these days. He murmurs her name as the familiar aching lump obstructs his throat. Alice. Alice. A feeling of desolation floods in and swamps him so that he slumps forward, covers his face with his hands and weeps.

forty-One

'What the heck you *doing* Jen?' Matty was staring at Jenna's hair. 'Cutting your flipping . . .'

'Not *me*, you div, it was *him*.'

'Who?' Matty pushed through the branches, squatted, gazed into her friend's face.

'Lassiter. He was here a second ago pretending to be Tarzan. He'd have cut it *all* off, I know he would, if you hadn't shown up.'

'What the heck *for*, Jen? Taking GCSE hairdressing, is he?'

Jenna stood up and bent over, knocking dead leaves and bits of twig off her skirt with her hand. She chuckled. 'Trust you, Mat. Only you could have me laughing seconds after some nutcase has threatened to poke my eye out with a pair of scissors.'

'He didn't!'

'He *did*, and he'd have done it too if I'd answered when you called.'

Matty shook her head. 'He wouldn't, not really. *Lassiter?* I mean, I know he's a rotten bully and all that, but poke someone's *eye* out? He's just a lad, Jen.'

Jenna snorted, dragging a comb across her head. 'So was

Billy the Kid, Mat.' She patted her hair. 'There – think my mum'll notice anything?'

Matty pulled a face. 'Probably.' She looked at her friend. 'You're not thinking of keeping quiet about this, Jen, surely?'

'What d'you mean?'

'Well, aren't you going to report him, get him done? You can't just let him get away with something like this.'

Jenna shook her head. 'You didn't *hear* him, Mat. Ned told me he was dangerous, possibly even mad, and I think he's right. He *sounded* mad. *Me Tarzan, you Jane*. What kid in his right mind . . .? He said if I looked round he'd pull your teeth out.'

'OK, so he's either bonkers or taking GCSE dental hygiene. All the more reason for you to grass him up, Jen.'

Jenna sighed, gazed at her friend. 'You don't *get* it, do you, Mat? I'm *scared*. He really frightened me, with his phoney voice and those jokey threats you could tell weren't jokey at all. The plain truth is, I *daren't* grass him up because I don't *want* my ears cropped or my eye poked out, and I don't want him practising his dentistry on you. No.' She shook her head. 'You and I are going to walk out of this chimp's nest in a minute like nothing's happened, Mat. You'll take your mum's bread home and say you had to queue. I'll say old Worldwide kept me back talking Internet, and if anybody notices my hair I'll say I got a wad of chewing-gum stuck in it and had to snip it out. OK?'

Matty shrugged. 'OK if you insist, Jen, but I'll tell you this: if that airhead tries anything on me – *anything* – I go straight to the Head *and* to my dad. Is *that* OK?'

Jenna pulled a face. 'Sure, if you think they'll be able to make out what you're saying with all your teeth gone.'

Forty-Two

'*Whatever* have you been doing to your hair, darling?' went Amy Finch, the instant Jenna walked in the kitchen.

Jenna grimaced. *Good old Mum, never misses a trick.* 'I got chewing-gum stuck in it, Mum. Had to snip it out.'

'*Chewing*-gum?' Amy slid the casserole back in the oven, closed the door and slipped off the padded glove. 'How on *earth* does a young woman, nearly fourteen years of age, manage to get chewing-gum in her hair? Did someone stick it on you during a scuffle?'

'No. I was tossing it in the air and catching it in my mouth and I sort of . . . missed.'

Amy's expression was that of someone who's just stepped in doggy-poo. 'Tossing it in the air and catching it in your *mouth*? I thought you were studying to become an airline captain, not one of those red-mouthed raucous women you see coming out of pubs at closing time, shrieking with laughter, surrounded by seedy men with greasy hair and suits that are shiny and don't fit.'

Jenna was forced to laugh. 'Oh *Mum*, you should see your face. I *am* going to be a pilot, and one of the things a pilot needs is co-ordination, which is what it takes to toss a wad of gum in the air and get your mouth under it. I was testing my co-ordination, see?'

'Yes, well.' Her mother sorted through the cutlery drawer. 'I'm sure the students at the Hampshire College of Aviation and Aeronautics have devised more elegant ways of testing their co-ordination, Jenna.' She smiled thinly. 'And besides, you missed. Perhaps the gum was trying to tell you something.'

'Aw yeah, as *if.*'

'Well, if a flagstone can have supernatural powers, darling, why not a wad of gum?'

Having no answer to this, Jenna went through to the hallway, draped her top over the banister, plodded upstairs and found Ned on the landing looking strained.

'You OK, Sis?'

'Yeah, why?'

'Where you been? You weren't with Matty Brewster.'

'What're *you* all of a sudden – my *shadow*? If you must know, Worldwide kept me talking and Matty couldn't wait. She had to get bread for her mum.'

Her brother's eyes searched her face. 'Sure it was Worldwide, Sis, not . . . someone else?'

'I *told* you.'

'Yes and I told *you*. I said he was dangerous, didn't I, and now you know. Or at least I think you do.' He shook his head. 'You're lucky it was only a bit of hair, Jenna. Now maybe you'll stop going on and on at me about . . . you know?'

'No I won't,' murmured Jenna. 'I don't know what it is he's dragging you into, Ned, but he's a total fruitcake so it's got to be something pretty stupid involving Grandad's gun, and if you *care* about Grandad, or Mum and Dad, or yourself, you'll tell Gavin Lassiter he's on his own. All you have to do is bring the gun back. Slip it to me. I'll get it to Grandad, and I won't tell him where I found it. Nobody will ever know. It's easy.'

'You think so? You come home late with a brand new hairstyle and you *still* think it's easy?' He snorted. 'It is for *you*, Sis. All you have to do is back off, but it's too late for me. I'm in and that's it.'

'Well I won't back off,' insisted Jenna, wishing she felt as brave as she sounded. 'I'm going to find out what you're up to, Ned. I'm going to get Grandad's gun back. And if something happens to me while I'm doing it, it'll be all your fault.'

Forty-Three

Her head was so messed up she had to force herself to tackle maths homework. It was trig, so she motivated herself by remembering what old Worldwide had said. *Aim to become a trig genius. A prodigy. The Robbie Williams of trigonometry.* She told herself that with a trial flying lesson in a few days she couldn't afford to screw around.

Later, with homework out of the way she lay on her bed with her eyes closed. A little camcorder inside her skull had videoed her after-school encounter among the rhododendrons and now it treated her to a replay. Tarzan in the Park, starring Jenna Finch and . . .?

That's a point, isn't it? I know Lassiter was the male lead but I never actually saw him. There's no proof, so I couldn't grass him up even if I dared.

The tape was a loop. As soon as Matty Brewster (best supporting actress) showed up and did her rescue bit, the whole thing started again. Jenna screwed up her eyes and shook her head and managed to dismiss it, only to find it replaced instantly by The Thing on the Landing, starring herself and introducing Ned Finch as the Thing. She groaned and let it run through to her closing lines. *I'm going to find out what you're up to . . . I'm going to get Grandad's gun back . . .*

Yeah but like, how? Ned's saying nothing. Lassiter certainly won't and anyway I daren't go anywhere near him. I've shadowed Ned and been caught at it. What next?

She lay watching the light fade, thinking. Gavin Lassiter was pressuring her brother into doing something bad. Ned's words proved it. *I'm in and that's that.* In what? Had to be a crime of some sort, didn't it? A crime with a gun. Murder? Her mind recoiled from that. A robbery then. An armed robbery. *Ned's always saying he's going to be a millionaire.* Where, though, and when? How could she stop it if she didn't know where or when? By taking the gun of course, but where was it? You can't take something you can't find.

Hey, what if . . .? She sat up. *What if Lassiter gets a letter? An anonymous letter that makes him believe the sender's on to him. Doesn't have to give any details. Just, I know what you're planning. Don't do it. Something like that. Might not work but it's worth a try, isn't it?* She rolled off the bed, crossed to her desk and switched on the computer.

Forty-four

She did it like a fax:

> To: Gavin Lassiter
> From: A friend

> *I know you are planning a robbery. I even know the name of your accomplice, and that you intend to use a gun. Unless you shelve this plan immediately I will tell the police and also the people you mean to rob. This is not a hoax.*

It *was* a hoax though. She couldn't go to the police without landing Ned and Grandad in big trouble, and she couldn't tell Lassiter's intended victims because she'd no idea who they were. Her only hope was that this letter would panic the nut into abandoning his plan.

She read it through, printed it out and folded it. She was about to shove it in an envelope when she hit a snag. *What's his flipping address?* The Lassiters hadn't been in Haverham long enough to be in the phone book. She couldn't very well ask Ned. The school would have it of course but there was nobody in school at this time of night, and anyway what excuse would she offer for wanting the information?

In desperation she used her mobile to call Matty. Luckily her friend was still up, with her phone switched on. 'Matty?'

'Jen, are you all right?'

'Yeah, listen. You don't happen to know Gavin Lassiter's address, do you?' She was speaking softly in case Mum or Dad overheard in passing.

Matty snorted. 'Why, you thinking of going round there, see if he fancies a night out?'

'Don't be stupid. I've written a note I hope'll scare him. I forgot I didn't have the address.'

'Yes, that *is* a slight snag but I can't help. Sorry.'

'Oh, well.' Jenna sighed. 'Just have to chuck it away, think of something else.'

'There are a couple of things you could do.'

'What?'

'You could wait till hometime tomorrow, follow him home and shove it through the letterbox.'

'Oh yeah, I can't *wait* to walk up that garden path, Mat. Especially if his folks're as crazy as he is.'

'Go for the other, then.'

'What's that?'

'Well, you know where his locker is 'cause he shares with Ned. You could stick the note in the nameplate where he couldn't miss seeing it.'

'But what if he shows up while I'm doing it?'

'Go early, eight o'clock.'

'And suppose Ned gets there before him?'

'Doesn't matter as long as he doesn't know who put it there. It's a printout, isn't it?'

'Yeah.'

'Well there you go then, it could be from anybody. He'll

pass it on to his charming friend, that's all. What's it say anyway?'

'Tell you in the morning, Mat. *If* I don't get caught.'

'You won't get caught at eight o'clock. Want me to come with you?'

'No I'll be OK, but thanks. See you tomorrow.'

'Yeah, see you. 'Night.'

''Night, Matty.'

forty-five

'Night. Not *good night.* They hadn't wished each other a good night and it wouldn't be. Not for Jenna anyway.

She lay for ages trying to sleep but thoughts kept bouncing around inside her skull and she couldn't. She heard Ned go to bed, then her parents. She heard the clock on the church tower strike eleven, then midnight, then one o'clock. *One o'clock – how the heck am I gonna get to school for eight when I haven't even closed my flipping eyes?* This wasn't strictly accurate: she'd had her eyes closed for ages but what happened was, her brain projected worrying movies on to the insides of her eyelids and the only way to avoid watching them was to lie with her eyes open. Even then she saw shoals of little lights floating in the darkness, and after a while her eyes smarted with tiredness.

And when she finally drifted off to sleep, some time after one, she found herself in a nightmare.

It is early morning, still dark, and she is at school, on the long corridor with the shiny floor and lines of lockers along both walls. There is nobody else in the building and it is dead quiet but she is scared, as if something is watching her. For some reason she is in her pyjamas and her feet are bare and the glossy linoleum feels like ice. Her right hand clutches an envelope she knows contains a dangerous secret.

She pads along the corridor, turning her head to left and right so she won't miss any of the names on the lockers. She is looking for a locker which might have Tarzan on it, or it might say another name followed by a line of letters and the words DENTAL SURGEON. *She has to deliver the envelope to this locker before anybody comes along and sees her. It is desperately important.*

The corridor is very long. So long in fact that when she pauses for a moment to peer ahead the two lines of lockers seem to meet in the distance. She begins to doubt she'll ever find the right one when a locker to her left suddenly begins to chime like a clock. In fact when she approaches it she sees that it isn't a locker at all but a grandfather clock. It has a glass door instead of a metal one and behind the glass, something moves. She hurries forward, knowing this is where she must deliver the envelope. Reflections on the glass prevent her seeing through it, and she is only a metre away when the door swings open to reveal Gavin Lassiter standing ramrod-straight inside with a gun in his hand, glaring down at her.

Her screams woke her and she lay trembling in damp, twisted sheets, not sure yet what was real and what was not. She heard footsteps and stared at the door and it wasn't Gavin Lassiter who flung it open, but her mother.

'Darling, whatever's the matter? We thought you were being murdered.'

'Oh, Mum, I've had such a *horrible* dream. A *nightmare.*'

'Ah, well . . .' Her mother plonked down on the bed, took Jenna in her arms and rocked her, murmuring into her hair. 'It's over, darling. You're safe and snug in your little bed and

Mummy's got you.' Jenna nodded and clung on. It was like being three again. Her father appeared in the doorway, looking tousled. 'Everything all right?' She felt Mum nod. 'Yes, Peter, it was just a nightmare. You get back into bed, I'll be there in a minute.'

She let Mum tuck her in, kiss her forehead. What she really wanted was to be held again while she told about the *real* nightmare: the one that started every time she woke up. *I can't though, can I?*

Her mother crept away. Small noises for a minute, then silence. Jenna lay wide awake, watching the little floating lights.

Forty-Six

As Jenna lay wakeful in the aftermath of her nightmare, her grandfather moaned and twitched in the throes of his.

He's been thinning lettuces: working his way along the row, pulling out all but the strongest seedlings, leaving each of these with several centimetres of space in which to grow. As he gets stiffly to his feet with a fistful of uprooted seedlings in his hand, he sees Rudyard ploughing through waist-high weeds towards his loft and has an idea. Instead of throwing the baby lettuces on the compost heap he'll take them round, offer them to Rudyard for his pigeons.

He sets off but makes slow progress, as if he's wading through treacle. By the time he reaches Rudyard's gate the old man has disappeared. Albert approaches the loft and hears somebody crying inside. Reluctant to barge in, he knocks softly. The door swings open by itself. On the ledge slumps Rudyard, weeping, his face covered by his hands. As Albert starts forward his boot comes down on something soft. He looks down. It's a dead pigeon. He sees that there are dead pigeons all over the floor. Something in a corner catches his eye. A familiar object. He tries to pretend he hasn't noticed it but his eyes refuse to obey him. He can't tear them away. There it lies, gleaming dully in the light from the open door. The gun.

'Aye, that's right,' chokes Rudyard through his veiny old hands. 'Your fault, Albert Larwood. If you'd left it in Palestine my birds'd be flying in the sunshine, not lying in the dust.'

'But I didn't . . . I mean, who . . .?' He indicates the carnage with a sweep of his hand.

'That lad o' yours,' croaks the old man, 'but he couldn't have done it without a gun and you supplied that. In the eyes of the law . . .'

'No!' His denial echoes round walls that seem to close in. The turbid air has feathers in it. He turns, choking, groping towards the door. As he passes Rudyard, the old man's hands slide down his face to reveal empty sockets, a fleshless skull. Albert's screaming lunge through the doorway hurls him headlong with a whump! into a cliff of grey feathers which dumps him on the seat of his pants then topples, burying him under an avalanche of choking down . . .

Forty-Seven

Two a.m. As Albert Larwood wakes gasping, one of Haverham's best known characters treads sedately over the Church Street cobbles, turning aside now and then to investigate an interesting scent. His name is Thomas, and the reason for his renown is that he spends most of his days snoozing on a chair in the Tourist Information Centre where there is warmth and the occasional saucer of milk, and where he suffers his ears to be tickled by fingers from all over the world. He may be just a black and white domestic moggy but he's often been photographed, and his name is mentioned fondly in Toronto, Tokyo and Tunbridge Wells. There's even a postcard in which Thomas can be seen curled in sunshine on the museum steps, fast asleep.

Tonight he's got the village to himself. He turns right, stalks down the ramp on to the car park and crosses it, sniffing the tyre of a dew-beaded van in passing. He's heading for West Lane in order to terrorize a tortoiseshell tom he knows. This tom is bigger and heavier than he is but Thomas is boss nonetheless. In fact at night Thomas is Lord of Haverham, fearing nothing that moves. The one thing he is afraid of never moves but he always gives it a wide berth anyway, though it's only a flagstone. He swerves round it now, the fur along his spine tingling from whatever it is the cold slab radiates. A big tortoiseshell is one thing; silent scentless invisible power quite another. Thomas hurries on.

Forty-Eight

'Bit early aren't you, love – twenty to eight?' Amy Finch was slotting bread in the toaster while Ned and Peter finished their branflakes. Jenna, dressed for school, turned in the doorway.

'Matty's mum got her these *really* expensive trainers, said if I came early she'd show me 'em.'

'Trainers?' Her father chuckled. 'I don't know how you stand the excitement, sweetheart, this time of morning.'

'And I expected a battle to get you out of bed at *all* after the disturbed night you had.'

'Disturbed?' Jenna frowned. She hardly ever remembered her dreams.

'Don't tell me you've forgotten your *nightmare*, darling. That scream must've roused the whole neighbourhood.'

'Oh ... oh yeah.' She nodded. *Lockers, hundreds of 'em, and an envelope. I remember now, and I know why I dreamed it too.* 'I remember a bit of it, Mum. It was daft.'

'*I* didn't hear anything,' growled Ned.

His mother shook her head. 'You sleep like the dead, darling. Always have.'

'Anyway,' said Jenna, 'I'm off. See you at teatime.'

The pavement gleamed damply and there was a chill in the air. She hurried along West Lane and up towards the car park, pausing as always before the aeroplane stone. As she looked down at the crudely executed engraving she became aware of a sense that she was making a mistake, that what she intended doing was not a good idea. Of course she'd been apprehensive all along, hence the nightmare, but until this moment she'd been resolute in her determination to carry out her plan. Now she was uncomfortably aware of the long white envelope in her pack with *Lassiter* on it in italics. It was as though she could *feel* it nestling against her back, though she knew she couldn't really. It was thin and light and contained a single folded sheet. It was easily the slimmest, lightest thing in a pack which held her mobile phone, a calculator, some crisps for breaktime and two fattish books, yet it seemed almost to be burning its rectangular shape on to her skin. It was ridiculous, but try as she might she could suppress neither the burning sensation nor the swelling sense of danger. It was only when she'd shrugged off the pack, dumped it on the ground and unzipped it that her agitation began to recede. She pulled out the envelope she'd pinned her hopes on, wanting only to be rid of it. A few metres away there was a post with a waste-bin clamped to it. She straightened up and went over to it, tearing and tearing till envelope and letter were reduced to a handful of ragged scraps which snowed down on the drink cans and chip trays in the bin.

She felt better straight away and stood for a minute taking deep breaths, wondering what on earth had come over her and how she was going to pass the time between now and school. Thomas the cat was making his way up the slope on his way to the Tourist Information Centre and his breakfast milk. Jenna saw that if he continued in a straight line he was bound to walk across the aeroplane stone but he didn't. Instead he swung left to avoid it, curved back onto his original course and padded past as if she wasn't there. She caught her lower lip between her teeth and shivered, gazing at the stone.

Forty-Nine

'So how'd it go, Jen?' enquired Matty. It was twenty to nine and Jenna had been in the schoolyard since five past eight.

She shrugged. 'It didn't.'

'How d'you mean it didn't? What happened?'

'I chickened out, Mat.' She'd had more than half an hour to decide what to tell Matty. *It was the aeroplane stone, it warned me. Made the letter hot so it was burning me through my pack.* She couldn't say that. It was the truth but Matty'd never swallow it. Laugh herself silly, more like. Easier just to say she was scared. She pulled a face. 'I had this nightmare. I was in the corridor, only it was like miles long with thousands of lockers, and when I found the right one Lassiter was inside. I woke up screaming and this morning I couldn't do it, simple as that.'

'Hmm.' Matty shrugged. 'Just have to think of something else, then.'

Jenna snorted. 'Wish I could think *about* something else Mat, like my flight. It's three days away, I should be jittering with excitement and all I can do is worry about Lassiter and that flipping gun. It's not fair.'

'No, it's not.' Matty laid a hand on her friend's shoulder.

'Don't let it spoil everything, Jen. I know it's easy for me to say, but something'll happen and it'll all sort itself out and anyway, none of it's *your* fault.'

Jenna smiled. 'Thanks, Mat, you're the best friend in the world, but if Ned's got the gun it's *all* my fault. If I hadn't nosed in Grandad's bedroom I wouldn't have seen it and mentioned it at home and Ned wouldn't even have known there *was* a gun.'

Matty shook her head. 'That's like saying it was her grandma's fault that Little Red Riding Hood got eaten by the wolf, Jen. If she'd stopped the kid visiting with baskets of goodies she wouldn't have been there on the fateful day. You can blame anyone for anything if you go back far enough.'

The pair might have gone on discussing blame if Laurence Pighills hadn't interrupted in typical style, tugging Matty's sleeve to get her attention. She jerked her arm free, scowling. 'What the heck's up with you, Piggo?'

'You'll never guess.' The boy's eyes shone with excitement.

'No, 'cause I won't *try*.'

'Well, you know that new lad in year nine? Gavin Lassiter?' Both girls nodded. He had their attention now.

'He's been caught nicking from lockers.'

Jenna's mouth went dry. 'When?' she croaked.

'This morning, about eight o'clock. Old Worldwide – you know he comes early, messes about with the computers? Well, he had to go up the corridor for something and there was this guy Gavin going along the lockers helping himself. Apparently he's got one of those whatsit – skeleton keys. They found a load of stuff in his bag. He's in Westerby's office now, waiting for the police.'

'Wow,' breathed Matty. She wasn't particularly surprised, but sounding impressed was the quickest way to get rid of Piggo.

He grinned, gleaming. 'Great, or what?'

Matty went 'Yeah,' and he scuttled off, bursting to tell somebody else. Matty looked at Jenna. 'Good job . . .'

'I know.' Jenna nodded, looking pale. 'I'd have got there before Mr Webb, *and* I'd have had that envelope in my hand with Lassiter's name on it.' She shivered. 'Just me and him, Mat, on that dark corridor. He'd probably . . . it's broken my dream, hasn't it? I never really believed all that till now.' *I didn't believe in magic stones either, but how else . . . ?*

Fifty

The school buzzed all day with versions of Lassiter's capture. He'd made himself so unpopular that most of the kids rejoiced at his downfall. Jenna certainly did, and she allowed herself to hope that this morning's events would put paid to whatever it was he'd been planning with Ned. She even managed to indulge in daydreams about her upcoming flight in Biology and R.E., two subjects she didn't think she'd need as an airline captain.

To everyone's disappointment, Piggo's information about the police turned out to be wishful thinking. Old Westerby, anxious as ever to preserve the school's good name, didn't call them. Instead he dragged in Lassiter's parents (they both had to take time off work), told them what their son had done and showed them the loot. They were a tough-looking couple and the Head expected defiance, refusal to believe, perhaps even violence. He was gratified instead to find them meek, apologetic and humble. When he mentioned Gavin's reputation as a bully, Mr Lassiter promised to take the lad in hand, and when he informed them that any further trouble would lead to Gavin's immediate expulsion, Mrs Lassiter thanked him for not involving the police and swore solemnly that from now on her son would be so good as to be unrecognizable.

As for the culprit, he sat the whole time on a hard chair outside the secretary's sliding window looking really, really penitent. Mrs Kershaw even saw him pull a hanky out a couple of times and dab his eyes. She assumed he was blubbing but he wasn't. In fact the whole thing was nothing but an act. A pose. He'd practised it loads of times, and why not? It cost nothing and saved a lot of hassle, and if some kid saw him like this and brought it up later in jest, well, it'd be the last jest that kid enjoyed for a while. You've got to be crafty to be a master criminal. Crafty and *hard*.

Fifty-One

When Jenna got in at ten to four Ned was in the kitchen scraping spuds. He must have practically run home, he hardly ever helped with the dinner, and Jenna told herself it was because he was off the hook with Lassiter. She could hardly wait to get him by himself so she could mention the gun, but Mum never left the kitchen till the meal was ready and Dad came home.

'Oh, Jenna,' said Mum as the four sat down. 'I nearly forgot. There's a package for you in the front room. From Grandad, I think.'

'Grandad?' *It must be something to do with Sunday.* She made to push back her chair.

Mum shook her head. 'Eat your dinner first, darling, it'll still be there when we've finished.'

To help the time pass, Jenna told her parents about Gavin Lassiter. As she spoke she watched Ned's face, but he was careful to keep it blank. When she'd finished, Dad looked across at him.

'You're pally with this guy aren't you, Ned?'

Ned shrugged and mumbled, 'Yeah, sort of.'

'Well, it's not a particularly good idea to get yourself

lumped in with the school delinquent. I'd sort of ease off if I were you, give him some space. You don't want a character like him dragging you down.'

'No, Dad.' Ned was staring at his plate, but Jenna could see that his face had turned pink. *He's wondering what Dad'd say if he knew* everything *about him and Lassiter.* The pinkness, too, she took to be a hopeful sign.

The minute pudding was over she excused herself and went through to the front room. The package lay on the coffee table. It was an A4 padded envelope with something hard and heavy in it. She took it up to her room and ripped it open. Inside was a stiff plastic folder like a writing-case with a big letter A on the front, and under it the words ACORNE SPORTS. In the folder was a fibre-tip pen, a booklet with a photo of a light aircraft on it, a pilot's log-book, a certificate, a folded sheet with a list of flying clubs in various parts of Britain, and the voucher itself. Grandad had scrawled on a post-it stuck to the voucher. *Now you know it's really going to happen, sweetheart*, it read.

'*Thanks*, Grandad,' whispered Jenna, flicking through the booklet. It was called YOUR GUIDE TO THE INTRODUCTORY FLYING LESSON, and had pictures and diagrams of aircraft and instruments. It reminded her of the Air Pilot's Manual she'd pored over at Keeley Library. 'I *do* know it's going to happen. I do. I just hope I can get this gun business over in the next couple of days so *you* can have a good day too.'

Fifty-Two

While Jenna sits on her bed examining the contents of her folder, Gavin Lassiter is doing his best to keep his bed between himself and his purple-faced, snarling father. Mr Lassiter has chased the lad upstairs in order to take him in hand, in fulfilment of the promise made to Mr Westerby. His eyes bug out as he glares at his son across the duvet. Flecks of spit fly out of his mouth when he speaks.

'I told you,' he splutters. 'I told you when we moved here, this was the last. The last time your mother and me'd ever let you force us to uproot ourselves and flit halfway across the flaming country just to get you out of scrapes of your own making. You're a criminal, Gavin. A nutter. I don't know where you get it from: nobody in my family ever got a kick out of hurting other people, robbing, torturing. Nobody in your mother's family either. I don't know where we went wrong, you've always had a good home, plenty to eat. We haven't abused you, neglected you, kicked you around, so how come you act the way you do, eh? Tell me that if you can, because I can't. Where'd we go wrong, Gavin?'

Gavin, half-scared, half-defiant, mumbles something unintelligible.

'Eh?' His father comes round the foot of the bed, one hand cupped to his ear. 'What's that you say? Too soft were we, not enough thrashings?' He lunges at the boy.

Gavin dives on the bed, rolls across it, stands up and shouts, 'I said you're boring, both of you. Boring, boring, boring, always have been, so I had to make things happen, didn't I? Had to get a life or die of boredom on the flipping settee, gawping at cook shows.' He flings out his arms, shrugs hugely. 'Why, Dad? Why naffing cook shows? What's the point of living if there's no excitement, no challenge? How can you build your lives round a bunch of sad geezers with names like Ainsley and Gary and Delia?' He snorts. 'And then you've the nerve to call me a nutter. You're the nutters, you and Mum, because you've chucked your lives away.'

'Yes, on YOU,' roars Lassiter senior. 'We've chucked 'em away on you, and what have we got to show for it, eh? Four different homes in five years and a ruddy psychopath in every one of 'em. Well I'll tell you this.' He inhales slowly, deeply, forces himself to speak more quietly. 'It's over, Gavin. Finito. Your mother and me, we don't want a son who thumps people, cuts 'em with modelling knives, chops bits off 'em. We don't want that sort of son any more, we'd rather have no son at all, so what I'm saying is, you pull one more stunt – one more of any sort – and I'll turn you in myself. And not just for that stunt, whatever it is. No, I'll tell 'em everything, right back to when you were eleven in Darlaston. The fire, remember?' He shakes his head. 'They'll put you away for ever, lad. Padded cell. And you needn't think we'll ever come to see you, your mum and me, 'cause we won't. We'll be too busy sitting on the settee, watching sad geezers with names like Ainsley and Gary and Delia, and we won't be on edge all the time, waiting for a knock on the door, wondering what our Gavin's done now.' He snorts. 'Because our Gavin, who won't be ours any longer, will

136

be so drugged up on tranquillisers he won't have done anything except what he always does, which is to sit like a cabbage on his lumpy little bed, gawping at the wall.'

He crosses the room, turns in the doorway. 'So think on. Model pupil, model citizen, or Broadmoor. Your choice.' He leaves, closing the door behind him.

Fifty-Three

Jenna had got to the last page of the booklet when she heard Ned on the stairs. She listened till his door closed, then went along and knocked.

'What d'you want?'

'Just a word. Can I come in?'

'OK but be quick, I've got homework.'

She opened the door, closed it behind her, looked at her brother. 'That stuff with Lassiter this morning. It changes things, right?'

'What d'you mean?'

'Well, he won't be going through with . . . whatever it was he was planning, will he? I mean, everybody'll be watching him.'

Ned shook his head. 'I dunno. He doesn't tell me everything, and anyway I haven't seen him since.'

'No, but it's obvious isn't it? *You* think it's off, I can tell.'

'How?'

'For one thing you're not jumpy, and for another you're doing your homework. It's days since you bothered with homework.'

'How d'you *know* that? Bugged my room, have you?'

138

'Don't be daft, I just know.'

'Think you know everything, don't you? What d'you want anyway?'

'You know what I want. Grandad's gun.'

'You still on about *that*? I told you I haven't got it. Don't know anything about it, so if that's all you've come about you might as well . . .'

The mobile warbled on his bedside unit. He picked up. 'Yeah? Oh hi, what's up?' He listened, scowling at Jenna, making motions with his free hand for her to leave. She shook her head and he said, 'Just a sec,' covered the mouthpiece with his palm and snarled, 'Get out *now*, Jenna, this is private.' He looked nervous.

Jenna snorted. 'Yeah, I bet it's private, and I bet I know who it is.' She raised her voice. 'It's Gav, isn't it? Gav the locker-knocker. How's it hanging, Gav?'

'Shut up, you *idiot*,' hissed Ned. 'You don't know what you're messing with.'

Jenna nodded. 'Oh but I *do*, Ned, that's the whole point. I know what I'm messing with, and I know what *you're* messing with too. Remember what Dad said: *I'd sort of ease off if I were you, give him some space.*' She sneered. 'I know what space *I'd* give him – six feet long, six feet deep, two feet wide, in the graveyard.'

She let herself out and trailed back to her room feeling depressed. *Thought it was sorted, didn't you, Jen? Happy for a bit there, weren't you?* She flopped on the bed and lay curled on her side, gazing at Grandad's folder and thinking how ecstatic she might have been right now if the Lassiters had never come to Haverham.

Fifty-four

Nine o'clock. Practically dark. Ned sits on the ledge in Rudyard's loft, waiting for Gavin Lassiter. He's not happy. Doesn't want to be here. Knows he ought not to be here, and definitely wants nothing to do with the terrifying enterprise his so-called friend has planned for a week tomorrow. I don't have to do it, *he tells himself.* I'll just say count me out. Or better still I'll take the gun, now, before he shows up. If he does it without the gun, there'll be nothing to connect him to me, will there? *The gun is five centimetres from the crook of Ned's knee, stuck to the underside of the bench with electrician's tape, but he makes no move to retrieve it. He won't be taking it and he knows he won't. Gavin Lassiter isn't a guy you can run out on. What was it he'd said, Tuesday night?* Two quick chops and you might as well have been born a monkey. *Ned shivers.*

He's sitting with his head down and his hands dangling between his knees when he hears Lassiter swishing through the weeds. He looks up as the door creaks open. 'Hi.' *He'd love to say* You're late *like Lassiter did last time, but he daren't.*

'Shove up.' Lassiter plonks himself down, forcing Ned to shuffle along a bit. It's part of showing who's boss. 'What's

up with you?' He looks sidelong at Ned.

Ned shrugs. 'Nothing. Why?'

'You've a face on you like a slapped bottom, what's the problem?'

'You needn't have grabbed my sister last night, cut her hair.'

'She was spying on you, Finch. Nobody spies on my people.'

'No, but her hair, Gav. Take weeks to grow back.'

Lassiter scoffs, fishing for cigarettes in his leather jacket. 'Not nearly as long as a thumb'd take, sunshine. Set of teeth.'

'Well I wish you'd leave her out, that's all.' It's weak and he knows it, but he knows too that he's alone in the dark with a dangerous guy.

Lassiter slips a cigarette between his lips, clunks the Zippo. Lighted from below his face looks evil. The cigarette wags as he speaks. 'Guy can't control his own sister, somebody's got to do it for him. You OK for Saturday?'

Ned sighs, nods. 'I suppose.' He looks at Lassiter. 'You know, I thought it'd be off after what happened this morning.'

'Ah!' The glowing tip of the cigarette bounces up and down in the dark. 'So that's what the miserable face is about: you thought you were off the hook after all. Well, old son,' he shakes his head, 'you couldn't be more wrong. All this morning's done is convince me it's time for yours truly to move along: say ta-ta to Mummy and Daddy and strike out on my own. Seek my fortune.' He laughs. 'Only I'm doing it the other way round: fortune first, then split. You don't catch me going out into the big wide world with a bit of bread and cheese in a spotted red handkerchief on the end of a stick and nothing in the old wallet.'

'So.' Ned watches the glowing tip. 'What time Saturday?' He's never felt so miserable. So scared. He wishes he'd been less quick to befriend the new boy last term: wonders how he

141

could've mistaken Lassiter's strangeness for something cool. Streetwise. Charismatic. His father's words replay inside his skull. His sister's words. I'd sort of ease off if I were you. *Oh sure. Say ta-ta to old Gavin and you're saying ta-ta to your thumbs as well, or your teeth, or both. Maybe even your sister.*

Not easy, Dad.

Fifty-Five

'Two days!' cried Matty as she came grinning out of her house Friday morning. 'How's it feel, Biggles?'

Jenna smiled. She didn't particularly feel like smiling, but Matty was so unfailingly chirpy you couldn't help responding. 'Gimme da woid an' I'm off like a boid,' she said.

'Hoo! She's a poet, doesn't noet.' They linked arms and swung down the street, weaving in and out of loitering kids.

Everybody was disappointed to see Gavin Lassiter in the yard. After his humiliation of yesterday they'd taken it for granted he'd wag off today: come slinking back after the weekend when the affair would be ancient history. But no, there he was, slouching on the steps with a ciggy in his gob like he'd never slumped outside Ma Kershaw's window with a hanky in his fist, blubbing.

As Jenna and Matty came through the gateway, a kid in year eight was passing the steps and happened to glance in Lassiter's direction. It was an innocent glance, but the bully was well aware what the kids were thinking. He needed to make an example of someone. This kid would do nicely.

'Who're *you* staring at, pigface?'

The kid looked up, startled. '*Me?* Nothing.'

143

'Oh.' Lassiter stood up. 'So I'm nothing, is that what you're saying?'

'N . . . no. I meant I wasn't staring.'

'So I'm a liar then?'

'I didn't say that.'

'So you *were* staring?'

'No, I just looked 'cause you were smoking.'

'Oh I *see*,' drawled Lassiter, sauntering towards the petrified boy. 'I was smoking and you thought, *I know: I'll report that guy, get him done*. Didn't you?'

'No.'

'Yes you did, you sneaky little scruff. Come *here*.' He lunged at the kid, grabbed a fistful of his hair. 'Know what happens to sneaks, do you? Dirty little sneaks who go whining to teacher, telling tales, getting other people into trouble? No? Then I'll give you a free demo.' He was holding the struggling kid with one hand, fishing in his pocket for something when a voice called out, 'Leave him alone, you plank.'

The bully turned. Gasps came from kids close enough to hear. Jenna held herself stiffly, trying to stop her legs from trembling. Matty moved a step closer to her friend, slid an arm round her waist. Lassiter gazed at Jenna.

'Did *you* say that, Finch?'

Jenna nodded. She daren't risk her voice.

'Plank, eh?' He giggled, an odd sound from somebody his size. 'Shall I tell you what happened to the last person who called me a plank, Finch?' He was still holding the kid, but seemed to have forgotten him.

'I expect you robbed his locker, Lassiter.' More gasps from the onlookers. The bully shook his head. 'Oh no, Finch, nothing so . . . painless. No: what happened was that a door slammed on the poor devil's hand. Heavy door it was,

144

oak with iron studs, eight hundred years old. He was good at art before, as well as calling people names. Useless at both, after. Oh, and by the way,' he smiled, 'I caught what you said last night, over your brother's mobile. *Locker-knocker*, wasn't it? Clever, that. Clever enough to call for special punishment. Come here.'

'Get lost.'

Lassiter snorted, twisted the kid's hair so hard he cried out. 'I said come here, or the kid gets it instead. Not fair I know, but that's life.'

The kid was crying. Jenna was about to obey when Miss Traynor's car turned into the yard. Miss Traynor taught girls' P.E. She saw Lassiter with the smaller boy, braked and wound her window down. '*You* again, Lassiter? Mr Westerby told me you were going to be a model pupil, starting today. You'd better let go of that boy's hair *now*, if you want to stay at this school.'

I don't want to stay: I'm not staying. It was on the tip of his tongue but he bit it back. *Not time yet. One more week.* He nodded, released his victim. 'Yes, miss. Sorry, miss.'

The kid shuffled off, nursing his scalp. Miss Traynor wound up her window and drove on.

Matty nudged her friend, giggled. *'Yes, miss. Sorry, miss.'*

Lassiter had moved away a bit, but turned as the teacher's car passed from sight round the building. 'Later, Finch,' he called. 'You too, Brewster.'

Fifty-Six

Later. The two girls were apprehensive for the rest of the day, especially at breaktimes, but they needn't have worried. Miss Traynor had had a word with old Westerby and he'd had a word with Gavin Lassiter. One hundred and fifteen words in fact. Here they are:

Miss Traynor tells me she saw you holding a boy by his hair, Gavin. A boy much smaller than yourself, who was crying. No, please don't bother to deny it, it's absolutely typical of you and Miss Traynor has perfect eyesight. I'm amazed that after yesterday's disgraceful episode, and bearing in mind the undertakings given to me in this room by both your parents, you feel able to persist in your bullying ways as if nothing has happened. I shall write to your father, inform him of this latest incident and warn him that one more transgression of any sort will lead to your instant expulsion. I assume you know what the word transgression means.

Gavin had replied with a single word, *Sir*, and had been sent back to his class. He wasn't easily scared but he was certainly afraid of his father. He spent the rest of the day wondering how to stop the silly old fool reading the Head's letter, and this drove all thought of Jenna and Matty out of his mind.

The two girls didn't know this, and at hometime they attached themselves to a group sauntering up Butt Lane and across on to Main Street. Even Lassiter wouldn't pounce in front of fifteen witnesses, every one of whom would give her left arm to see him in further trouble. Before parting, the pair arranged to meet up at ten next morning for a busride into Keeley to look at clothes, CDs and lads. It was something to look forward to, and in fact would prove considerably more interesting than usual, though they didn't know this either.

Fifty-Seven

'Will you be home for lunch, darling?' Saturday morning, nine fifty. Amy Finch tidying the front room, Jenna getting into her zippy leather jacket.

Jenna shook her head. 'Thought we'd grab something at Burger King if that's all right, home for tea.'

Her mother pulled a face. 'It's all right, I suppose, but it beats me what you find to do in Keeley all day.'

'There's *loads* to do, Mum. Look at all the clothes shops for a start, then there's Virgin, Our Price, Boots and Smiths to check out for CDs and videos. There's Sunwin, the market, the precinct, the library, the park. You can't *do* it all in a day.'

'Well, darling, all I can say is rather you than me. Just make sure you're home in daylight, and be *careful.*'

Jenna smiled, patted a bulging pocket. 'You can always call me if you're worried, you've got my number.'

Amy shook her head. 'You and your mobile. I shan't go to those lengths, only stay out of trouble. Oh, and d'you think you could pop into Asda for me at some point, pick up one of those crusty baguettes?'

'I'll try to remember, Mum. See you.'

Matty was at the bus shelter. 'Remind me,' said Jenna, 'to call at Asda just before we leave Keeley.'

Matty nodded. 'Why just before we leave?'

''Cause I've to get a flipping baguette and you know what they're like: about a metre long. I'd look a total div trailing one of those around all day.'

They caught the ten ten along with a lot of other people. Neither girl mentioned Gavin's threat of yesterday but it was in both their minds. Today they'd make sure there were always plenty of people around. No short-cuts across derelict land, no lonely spots.

They did all the usual things. It was a chilly day but dry so they could flaunt their kit: no need to carry umbrellas or dash from doorway to doorway. At half-twelve they shared a table at Burger King with two of their friends, after which the four of them made a leisurely round of clothes shops in the mall. In quiet moments, Jenna tried to blot out Lassiter by thinking about her flight tomorrow, but she caught herself looking out for him all the same. She couldn't help it.

At half-four Matty reminded her about Asda. The other two girls didn't want to go there so they left, and Matty and Jenna sauntered along to the supermarket. The car park was still pretty full.

'What a bummer,' grumbled Jenna, 'having to queue at the checkout for one flipping item. I should've tried some of the bread shops.'

'Nah.' Matty shook her head. 'Bread shops don't do baguettes, Jen. Not the long ones anyway.'

'Three short ones'd be just as good,' growled Jenna, 'unless Mum's gonna use it to poke things out from behind the fridge or something.'

Matty nodded. 'That could be it, you know. *Tips from the*

professionals: a baguette makes a perfect device for poking stuff out from behind a fridge, under a double bed: even that awkward space inside the piano.'

Jenna giggled. 'Idiot.' They entered the store. Jenna picked up a basket. They wove through slow-moving customers towards the bread aisle. The baguettes stood in a round wire rack at the end of the aisle. Jenna yanked one out like King Arthur pulling the sword from the stone. The basket was too short so she abandoned it and joined a queue with the bread tucked under her arm. Every few minutes the queue shuffled forward a bit. It was hot in the store. Jenna grew bored. She started picking scabs of crust off the baguette and chewing them. Matty laughed. 'Your mum's gonna murder you, Jen. What's the point of crusty bread once the crust's gone?'

Jenna didn't reply. She was watching a security man who had come in and was heading for the stairs. He was wearing a blue crash-helmet and carrying a black metal box like a small suitcase. An armoured truck was parked outside. Jenna could see the driver in his cab. The store closed at half-five so they must have come for the day's takings. The man disappeared upstairs. The queue shuffled forward. The woman in front of Jenna was packing. Jenna laid the baguette on the belt and was fishing a pound out of her purse when Matty dug her in the side and hissed, 'Look.' She looked.

Gavin Lassiter was loitering near one of the sliding doors. Beyond him, leaning on the rail of a trolley-park not far from the armoured truck, was Ned.

Fifty-Eight

'Oh God, no!' gasped Jenna, pressing the fingers of both hands to her mouth. 'They're not ... surely they're not gonna ...?' *He was here the other day, hanging around. I wondered why and now it's obvious. The day's takings.* 'Mat – what do we *do*? We can't just ...'

'Sssh!' Matty nodded towards the stairs. 'Look.' The security man was coming down, tilted over to the right as though his box was heavier now. He strode past the checkouts heading for the exit. Lassiter wasn't there, must have gone outside. The door slid open. The man walked out, strode towards the truck. *Now*, thought Jenna, *they'll do it now*, but nothing happened. She couldn't see Ned by the trolley-park. The man went to the back of the truck. A hatch opened. *Now, then*. The man shoved his box through the hatch. The hatch closed. The man came round to the passenger side. The door opened. He clambered up, slammed it shut. The truck rolled forward. Nothing had happened. There was no sign of Ned or Lassiter. Jenna let out a long sigh. The checkout girl passed the baguette's barcode across the sensor, glanced up. 'You all right, love?'

'What?' Jenna looked at her. 'Oh yeah, thanks, I'm fine.'

She handed over the coins, picked up the bread. The girl gave Matty the change. They walked to the exit. Outside there was no Ned, no Lassiter. Enormously relieved, Jenna shook her head. 'So what the heck were they *doing*, Mat?'

Matty pulled a face. 'That's easy, Jen,' she murmured. 'We've just watched a rehearsal.'

Fifty-Nine

Seven-thirty. Ned and Lassiter in Rudyard's loft. It's the last day of April and the evenings are drawing out. Lassiter is speaking.

'OK, let's go through it again. The truck turns in to the car park at five fifteen. Where are you?'

Ned sighs. They've been over this four times in the last half hour. 'I'm by the trolley-park nearest the building.'

'What've you got?'

'I've got a line of four trolleys ready to go.'

'And what're you doing now?'

'I'm fiddling with the strap, pretending to add more trolleys to the line.'

'OK. The truck's crossed the car park and stopped. The guard gets out and goes into the store. What do you *not* do?'

'I don't watch him. I keep my head down, work at the trolleys.'

'What if a customer comes for a trolley?'

'I let her take one, don't let her see my face.'

'And what if hers is the last trolley in the park?'

'I let her take it, collect some from another park. I have six minutes.'

'What if you run into a real trolley-collector?'

'I won't: they're ordered round the back at five to clean up the delivery bays. They clear the parks after the store closes.'

Lassiter nods. 'OK. So let's assume everything goes smoothly. Six minutes go by, you're watching the window and you see the guard coming towards the exit with the box. What do you do?'

'I get my four trolleys lined up. I've already checked to make sure none of 'em has a dodgy wheel 'cause when it's time for 'em to move, they've got to move fast.'

'Right, so the guy comes round the back of the truck. Then what?'

'I start trundling my trolleys, showing no interest, like there's no truck there at all.'

'And?'

'I'm about five metres from the guy when the driver operates the hatch. As it starts to open I speed up and ram the guard as hard as I can with the trolleys, knocking him sideways. You step from behind a parked car with the gun and tell him to hand over the box, while I run with the trolleys and tip 'em over on their sides across the doorway to delay anybody who might have seen what's happening from inside. I bumble about, pretending I'm trying to pick up the trolleys but actually making things worse, and when people start showing up I run. By then you've got the box and split. I go home, don't try contacting you, show up at school Monday as if nothing's happened. If you're not there I carry on as normal, wait for you to contact me. When the robbery's on radio and in the paper I show interest, but no more than anybody else.' Ned shrugs. 'That's it.'

'That's it, Finch,' purrs Lassiter, 'except for one thing.' He gazes into Ned's troubled eyes. 'Over this next week, and especially when you're actually doing the job, remember the little story I told you: you know, the one about thumbs?' He lays a hand on his accomplice's shoulder, grins in the gathering dusk. 'It'll help keep you loyal.'

154

Sixty

What you gonna do, *Jen?* Matty had asked this question when the two girls were parting outside her house at six o'clock. Jenna hadn't been able to answer it then and she couldn't answer it now. It was half past nine, she'd got into trouble for being late for tea and for picking bits off the baguette, and now she was trying in vain to get her homework out of the way so she could enjoy her birthday tomorrow.

Some hope. She chewed her pencil, staring out across the dark garden. *I know what I* should *do,* she thought. *I should tell Mum or go to the police. I've no excuse now: I know what Lassiter's planning, except I don't know which day. Matty reckons it's got to be a Saturday because he and Ned rehearsed on Saturday. She thinks it's set for next week and I bet she's right.*

It didn't make things any easier though. Ned and Grandad would still be in terrible trouble if she told what she knew: she might as well have told in the first place. *And what about tomorrow? My birthday. My flying lesson. What happens to all that if I tell and they come for Ned?*

She knew the answer to that one all right. It'd be off.

Finito. No birthday, or at least none that anybody would notice, and no trial flying lesson. Instead there'd be shock, tears and shame. Everything would be ruined. Everything.

Yes, but still, I can't just let it happen, can I? For one thing it's an offence to know about a crime and not tell the police. I could go to jail, never mind Ned. And what about Matty? She knows too. She's waiting to see what I'll do. I can't say to her, Oh, I decided to let it go ahead rather than mess up my birthday.

She groaned, threw down her pencil and buried her face in her hands. This whole thing was too big. Too big for her to handle by herself, even though she was nearly fourteen.

OK listen. Say there was somebody, right? Somebody older, from outside the family. What might she say? Mightn't she say, Look, to the best of our knowledge this robbery is planned for next Saturday, so it isn't going to make any real difference whether we tell the police now or wait till Monday morning. The only difference is, if we wait till Monday we won't wreck your birthday. *Yeah, I think she might say that. I mean, I know it's selfish putting myself first, but I'm not exactly going to have a carefree birthday, am I? It's going to be on my mind the whole time like it has been for days, taking the edge off everything. So that's what I think I'll do. Hang on till Monday. Thirty-six hours can't be that important, and it'll make all the difference to me. Better tell Mat.*

She reached for her mobile, punched in Matty's number.

Sixty-One

Happy Birthday to you
Happy Birthday to you
Happy Birthday, dear Jenna
Happy Birthday to you.

Mum, Dad and Ned, singing at the breakfast table. Nobody was ever going to offer them a recording contract but it was sort of nice, as long as you didn't let yourself think about certain stuff that was waiting to happen.

Jenna grinned, blushed and nodded. 'Thanks.'

Her father smiled at her. 'How's it feel to be fourteen, sweetheart?'

She shrugged. 'Same as thirteen, so far.'

'Ha! You wait till forty. Not like thirteen then, worse luck.'

'Aren't you going to open your presents, darling?' her mother asked. There were three packages by her plate.

Jenna nodded. ''Course.' She picked them up one by one, read the labels. *Love Mum and Dad. Luv'n'stuff, Ned. Lots and lots of love, Auntie Laura.* She felt a pang of sadness as it struck her there was no package with Grandma's writing on it, nor would be ever again. Then she thought about

Grandad's present, waiting for her out at the Aeroplane Club, and the moment passed.

Mum's and Dad's present was a jacket she'd seen in Kit to Die For. Black denim, pockets everywhere. She must have mentioned it and Mum had remembered. Auntie Laura had sent a huge soft Snoopy wearing goggles and an old-time pilot's helmet, so Dad had obviously dropped a hint of some sort to his sister. Ned's was a book, and when she tore off the giftwrap and read the title she got a lump in her throat. SISTERS IN THE SKY it was called, and it was a collection of true stories of famous women pilots. This from the brother who'd said *nobody'd fly in a plane with a captain who might be gawping at herself in the mirror*. The brother she'd probably send to jail tomorrow.

'Thanks, Ned,' she croaked. 'It's . . .' She gathered the gifts in her arms. 'They're all just *perfect*.' Then she burst into tears.

'Darling.' Mum came round and held her. 'What on earth's the matter? This is supposed to be a happy day for you. Is something wrong?'

And of course she couldn't tell: burbled something about everybody being so kind to her when she didn't deserve it. Ned knew though. He ruffled her hair on his way past, mumbled that he'd better go change before Grandad showed up. She got it under control after a minute or two and went up to wash her face. *Mustn't spoil this day, whatever happens after. Got to be happy for Grandad.*

He was coming at half-nine in the car. Jenna would ride with him and they were calling for Matty. Ned was travelling with Mum and Dad. The airfield was nine miles away and her lesson was due to start at eleven.

By the time they were on their way, genuine anticipation had crowded everything else out of Jenna's mind so that she didn't need to pretend. Grandad had his foot down, trying to stay in touch with his son-in-law's Volvo. The two girls clung on to the edge of the back seat, exchanging looks of mock terror as the old Micra sped along the road.

Matty grinned. 'Flying's gonna seem tame after this, Jen.' She glanced into the old man's mirror. 'Can this thing loop the loop, Mr Larwood?'

Grandad shook his head. 'No, but that's an ejector-seat you're sitting on. Want a demo?'

The Keeley and District Aeroplane Club was housed in a one floor concrete building a few metres from the airfield's perimeter track. They parked the cars beside it and went in, following a RECEPTION sign. Grandad led the way because he'd been here before. Jenna followed. Her heart was racing because she'd spotted a blue and white Cessna parked on the apron in front of the club's hangar. She knew her lesson was to be in a Cessna, so this might easily be the one. The dream was coming alive.

The Finch family crowded into a small office with blowups of old planes round its walls. A young man smiled at them across a counter. 'Miss Finch, is it: Jenna Finch?' His blue and red tie had a pattern of pilot's wings on it.

Grandad ushered her forward. 'Y . . . yes,' she managed to stammer, 'that's me.' *He must be a qualified pilot.*

'Good. My name's Dan, by the way. How are you today, Jenna? It's your birthday isn't it?'

'I'm fine thanks, and I'm fourteen today.'

'Fourteen and bursting to fly.' Dan smiled. 'Well Jenna, there's just a bit of paperwork to see to before you meet your instructor.' He looked at the others. 'I'll need Mr Larwood: everybody else might like to go through to the bar till we get the boring bit done.' He indicated an open door. 'There's coffee, tea, some stronger stuff. We'll call you when it's time.'

Mum, Dad, Ned and Matty went through to the bar. While Grandad and the young man attended to some forms, Jenna leaned on the windowsill looking out. Two people were pulling another Cessna out of the hangar by means of a rod attached to its nosewheel. You could tell it was light because its wings rocked slightly as it moved. *Like a butterfly*. This one was cream and red.

'Jenna?' The young man's voice. She turned. A tall man was standing by the counter. Dan nodded towards him. 'Jenna, this is Ronald Freeman who'll be taking you up today. Ronald, meet Jenna Finch, your P.U.T.' The tall man smiled, stuck out a hand. 'Hello Jenna, good to meet you.'

They shook hands. 'What's a P.U.T.?' asked Jenna.

'Pilot under training,' said the instructor.

Jenna goggled. 'Is that *me*?'

Freeman nodded. 'Certainly it's you. Today's lesson will be entered up in your pilot's log and counts towards the flying hours you need to qualify for the P.P.L.'

'P.P.L.?'

'Private Pilot's Licence.' He smiled. 'I'll just call A.T.C., then we can walk out to the aircraft.'

'Air Traffic Control,' said Dan, before Jenna could speak. She smiled, nodded.

The instructor went over to the phone. Grandad looked at Jenna. 'All right, sweetheart?'

'Oh, yes.'

'Not nervous or anything?'

'No. Well, a bit I suppose. I didn't know it was ... you know, a *real* flying lesson.'

'Oh, yes.' The old man winked at Dan. 'It's real all right.

160

They don't screw around at the Keeley and District Aeroplane Club; that right, Dan?'

''Sright, Mr Larwood.' Dan nodded.

Freeman hung up, turned. 'OK young woman, off we go.' He strode to the door, Jenna at his heels.

'Tell the others, Grandad,' she called.

'I will,' chuckled the old man.

'Good luck,' said Dan.

She followed the tall man through a gate in a wire fence and across the perimeter track towards the blue and white Cessna. *So I was right*. Her instructor stopped in front of the plane, looked at her. 'Have you flown in a light aircraft before, Jenna?'

She shook her head. 'Just airliners, but I've flown a Cessna on simulator.'

'*Have* you now?' He arched his brow. 'Do you intend learning to fly then, someday?'

'Oh yes, it's my greatest ambition, only . . .'

'I know what you're going to say, Jenna. Money, right?'

She nodded. 'Thirty thousand pounds. I can't see how I'll ever . . .'

'Thirty *thousand*?' Freeman shook his head. 'Not for a P.P.L. Six thou, I reckon. Seven at the outside.' He grinned. 'Still a lot of dosh, I know. Anyway, let's get you started and we'll see what happens.'

They did what the instructor called a walk-round inspection, checking control-surfaces, tyres, lights. He seemed pleased that Jenna knew about rudder, elevators, ailerons and flaps. 'Nice to have a first-timer who's done her homework,' he smiled. 'Come on: let's get airborne.'

He opened the left-side door, boosted her up, helped her strap herself in. She looked at the instrument panel. It was just like the one on *Flight Simulator*. Six dials. She

161

whispered their names as her instructor walked round to his door. *Air Speed Indicator. Attitude Indicator. Altimeter. Turn Indicator. Heading Indicator. Vertical Speed Indicator.* He must have seen her lips moving because he smiled as he slid into his seat. 'Know the instruments, do you?'

Jenna nodded. 'Their names. I'm not sure how to use them.'

'That's what *I'm* for, Jenna: to teach you how. Here: put this on.' He handed her a headset. She put it on and he leaned over, adjusting the mike. 'That's so we can talk to each other when the engine's on.' She nodded and he said, 'I think your family's waiting for a wave.' She looked through the window. They were standing in a line beyond the wire fence. She lifted a hand, feeling like Amy Johnson arriving at Darwin. They all waved back.

Sixty-Two

With its engine running the little plane vibrates, filled with noise. Jenna peers through the wind-shield, watching the blur of the propeller. Freeman's voice crackles in her headset as he talks to A.T.C. She tries to listen but can't make out what's being said. There's a burst of engine noise and they're moving: rolling across the apron towards the perimeter track. It isn't anything like taxiing in an Airbus or a Boeing, where you only know you're moving because the buildings seem to be sliding backwards. The tiny Cessna bumps and sways as though buffeted by a high wind. This is something you don't get on simulator, and Jenna is so struck by the apparent fragility of the aircraft that she speaks aloud without meaning to. 'A butterfly,' she murmurs, 'it's just like a butterfly.'

Her instructor chuckles. 'Know what you mean, Jenna, but they're unbelievably strong, these light aircraft. Flight subjects 'em to tremendous stresses, but they're designed to stand up to far more than they'll ever have to cope with. You may feel as though you're strapped to a butterfly, but you're a damn sight safer in this little beauty than you'll ever be in a car. Give 'em another wave, eh?'

Jenna looks out. The Cessna is rolling along the perimeter track no more than five metres from the fence. She can see the smiles on everybody's faces as they watch her go by. There are several strangers as well as her own party. She waves and they all wave back, even the ones who don't know her. It's as though being in this aircraft has somehow turned her into somebody special.

Freeman is talking to her about steering on the ground, taxiing procedures. She's sort of listening, but her excitement has her gazing about her at other aircraft, painted markings on the tarmac, the control tower, the clouds. The Cessna stops and the instructor tells her they're awaiting permission to take off. 'Rest your hand lightly on the control wheel,' he says, 'and let your feet touch the rudder-pedals. We call this following through. It lets the student get a feel of how the attitude of the aircraft is governed by our gentle manipulation of these controls. Everything is done gently: there's never a need to yank or shove or stamp.'

Jenna, heart thumping, caresses the wheel. They seem to wait ages, though it's probably only a minute or two. Voices quack and crackle in Jenna's ears. The propeller whirrs. The Cessna's wings rock in the breeze. Then they're moving again, out on to a runway which seems tremendously wide, viewed from this tiny plane.

'OK, here we go.' Freeman eases forward the throttle. The engine snarls and the plane rolls forward, gathering speed. 'Watch your instruments,' says the instructor. 'We get airborne at around eighty-five knots.' Jenna tries to keep her eyes on the clock, but they keep being drawn through the windshield and the arc of the propeller to the blur of concrete which races towards them and vanishes underneath. With the instrument's needle hovering round the eighty-five mark she feels a slight push through her thighs and bottom. The ribbon of runway sinks beneath the aircraft's nose and she's seeing the roofs of buildings to her left. Ahead the ground has disappeared completely as the Cessna climbs towards the clouds.

'Look left,' drawls Freeman. 'D'you see your family?'

She peers down. It's hard to recognize things from up here but yes: there's the club building, some parked cars, people, faces upturned, by the fence. 'Yes,' she cries, 'there they are.'

'OK, but remember to keep your hands and feet on the controls.'

'Oh . . . sorry, I forgot.'

He chuckles. 'Understandable. Look at your altimeter, tell me our current altitude.'

'Is it . . . six hundred feet?'

'Spot-on, Jenna. Excellent. We'll climb to two thousand, then get on course. You live at Haverham, right?'

'Yes.'

'OK. What direction's Haverham from the airfield, d'you know?'

Jenna thinks for a moment. 'It's north isn't it, or northwest?'

'Nice try. It's northeast. Shall we go take a look at it?'

At two thousand feet you can see Haverham church tower on the horizon. Freeman turns the Cessna's nose towards it and shows Jenna how pilots use the horizon on a clear day to keep the aircraft flying straight and level. He makes her hold the wheel and rest her feet on the rudder pedals. Then, quite casually he drawls, 'You've got it.'

For a moment she doesn't understand. It's only when her instructor raises his arms and clasps his hands behind his head that the penny drops. Oh God, I'm flying the plane.

'Just relax,' murmurs Freeman. 'Don't grip the wheel tightly like that. Nothing bad's going to happen. Watch the horizon, keep it in the same position relative to the windshield and you'll maintain level flight. That's it.'

Jenna inhales slowly to make herself relax. She watches the

165

horizon. The church tower has sunk below it now but the white flag of St George fluttering from its pole helps her keep it in sight. Her heart is kicking her so hard in the ribs she keeps expecting it to jog the plane off course, but on it flies. And I'm the pilot, the pilot, the pilot.

'Notice the tower, Jenna,' murmurs her instructor. 'It's a touch to our left now, so you need to ease the wheel very slightly to the left. Least little bit of pressure, that's it. Now gently right till it's central again. There. Tower's dead ahead, you've made your first course correction and I've got it.'

He has control. Jenna lets out a long breath, stretches her arms. A warm glow suffuses her and she can't keep from smiling. I've made my first course correction. Wow!

'Yes, and it was very well done.' Startled, she looks at him. It's as if he's read her mind. He's smiling broadly. 'No Jenna, I'm not psychic. I remember my own first lesson, that's all.' He chuckles. 'Most students overcorrect at first. You didn't, though that might have been nothing but a fluke. Time will tell. Now I'm going to put us into a sixty-degree bank and I want you to find your house for me.'

The plane tilts so steeply to the left that Jenna grabs the wheel. 'It's OK,' growls Freeman, 'you won't fall out. D'you recognize anything?'

Feeling daft, she lets go the wheel and peers down. At first it's all a jumble, like the street-plan of somebody else's town, but she makes herself look more carefully and soon identifies Rawdon Road by its width. This enables her to find Butt Lane and the school, then Main Street, which she follows with her eyes up to the church. There's the museum, so that must be the car park. From the car park it's a simple matter to find West Lane and to identify the row of houses which includes her home. 'There.' She jabs her finger at the window. 'That terrace, house with the aerial dish.'

Freeman nods. 'I see it. Looks a nice spot.'

'It's OK. Can we fly over my grandad's, please? It's at Marsh.'

'Which way's Marsh?'

'Oh . . . that way, I think. Yes, this looks like Marsh Lane.'

And in five seconds there it is, a thousand feet below. The hamlet of Marsh, Grandad's cottage, the allotments. She recognizes old Rudyard's pigeon loft and pinpoints Grandad's plot from it. 'There,' she points, 'that's my grandad's allotment.'

'Likes things neat and tidy then, your grandad?'

'Uh . . . I suppose.' A picture flashes through her mind of Grandad's living room, messy since Grandma died, but she can see what Freeman means. Square, weedless beds in a grid of straight paths, seedlings in immaculate rows.

'Seen enough?'

'Oh yes, thanks.'

'Good. I'm taking us back to two thousand, then we'll do some upper air work.'

Jenna knows what upper air work is because she's read about it. She's even done some on simulator. The Cessna climbs, then levels out. 'OK, Jenna.' Freeman folds his arms. 'You've got it.'

In the next half hour he talks her through some basic manoeuvres: nose-up attitude, nose down, bank left and right, bank and turn, maintain level flight using landmarks and the horizon. Presently he points to a tiny feature on the skyline. 'That's our control tower. I want you to steer towards it.'

'Are we going home?'

He nods, smiling. ''Fraid so, Jenna. Passes quickly, doesn't it?'

'Too quickly.' She glances at him, her heart in her mouth. 'D'you think . . . I could be a pilot?'

'Don't see why not. You came prepared and followed my

167

instructions. You've a nice touch on the controls and you don't seem nervous at all.' He pulls a face. 'Lot more to it than we've done today of course: months of study at groundschool and in your own time: navigation, meteorology, radio procedure, air law, plus hours and hours of upper air work, approach and landing, emergency procedures, etcetera, etcetera, etcetera.' He grins. 'Apart from that it's a doddle.'

She grimaces. 'That and the money. Still,' she brightens, 'Amy Johnson made it, and her instructor told her she was useless after her first lesson.'

'Well there you are. One thing's absolutely certain, Jenna: if you want to fly, and I mean really want it, you'll find a way.'

They're circling the airfield, Freeman talking to A.T.C. Jenna watches the runway rise to meet them, not wanting this to end, willing the little Cessna to stay airborne, stay airborne. Clinging on to the very very end of flight.

Sixty-Three

They fussed round her as she and Freeman came through the gate, slapping her on the back, ruffling her hair, punching her in the arm. The words ace, Biggles and wizard prang were uttered. Pink with a blend of pleasure and embarrassment, Jenna ducked and dodged while her instructor, wearing a tolerant smile, sidestepped the sort of mêlée he'd clearly seen before.

'How'd it go, sweetheart?' asked Grandad as they started moving towards the clubhouse.

'Oh, Grandad, it was bad, wicked and fabulous all rolled into one. I wished it'd never end. I don't know what I'll do if I can't fly again, keep *on* flying. It's a whole other world up there and it's *mine*; where I belong.'

Her grandfather laughed. 'So as a birthday present it wasn't a total flop, then?'

'Flop?' She flung her arms round him, hugged him tight. 'It was the wickedest birthday present anybody ever had, and you're the coolest grandad on the planet earth.'

'Well,' the old man's voice cracked a bit and his eyes seemed moist, 'at the risk of losing that title, I have to mention some paperwork that's waiting for the two of us at

Reception.' He looked at the others. 'Why don't you all go back to the bar and toast Jenna's birthday in a drop of something nice while we complete the formalities?'

Dan smiled from behind the desk. 'How was it, Jenna?'

'It was so great it's unbelievable.'

Dan nodded. 'Your instructor was well impressed too. He told me.'

'Did he, Dan, *really*?'

'Yes, really. *Natural aptitude* were his actual words.'

As Grandad bent over the form he was filling in, Jenna said, 'We flew right over your allotment, Grandad. I knew it was yours because of the old pigeon loft next door. Mr Freeman said it was very neat and tidy.'

The old man grunted. 'How high were you?'

'A thousand feet.'

'Ah well that's it, isn't it? Weeds don't show from a thousand feet.'

Dan overheard and laughed. 'I bet it *is* neat and tidy though. *My* grandad had an allotment and it was always immaculate. His pride and joy, that bit of garden was.'

The old man signed at the foot of the form, slid it to Dan. 'Talking about the pigeon loft's reminded me, Jenna. I saw your brother poking about up there the other day, meant to mention it to him. I will too before the day's out.'

Jenna's heart lurched violently enough to make her gasp. Her grandfather looked at her.

'What's up, sweetheart?'

'N . . . nothing, Grandad. Bit of hiccups. The excitement I suppose.' *The pigeon loft. Of course*, that's *where it is. Why the heck didn't I think of it, it's so obvious*?

'Aye, that'll be it, right enough. Well,' he smiled, 'all good things come to an end, young Jenna.' He looked at Dan. 'We'll be off then. Thanks for . . .'

'Oh just a minute, Mr Larwood, I'm sure Mr Freeman'll want to say goodbye.' He went through a doorway and reappeared a moment later with the tall instructor, who strode forward and stuck out his hand. 'Goodbye for now, Jenna, it was a pleasure flying with you, and remember what I said: if you really want it, you'll find a way.'

'I won't forget,' said Jenna, though her mind was now on something far less pleasant. Freeman shook hands with her grandfather and then they left the clubhouse, picking up the others on the way. As they emerged, the cream and red Cessna was taxiing along the perimeter track. Jenna followed it with her eyes, wishing she was going where it was going and not to old Rudyard's pigeon loft.

Sixty-Four

Ned sits in the Volvo's backseat gazing dully at the backs of his parents' heads. The buzz of Jenna's birthday treat has blurred his worries for a while, enabling him to get into the spirit of the occasion. The look on his sister's face when she came through that gate lifted his heart so high that tears came to his eyes, though he managed to hide this from the others.

Now it's all spoilt. Walking to the cars, Grandad had sidled up close to him and murmured, 'Spotted you going into old Rudyard's loft last Wednesday evening, lad. Not getting up to mischief in there, I hope.' He'd done it so nobody else heard, which was something.

Mischief. If you only knew. 'No, Grandad, I'd been thinking about the place: you know, how me and Jenna used to watch the birds through the fence when we were little, and I decided to see what it was like now.' What a smooth liar, it's associating with Gav I suppose. Wish the creep was dead.

Grandad had only grunted so Ned thought that was that, but then the old man had mentioned Jenna recognizing the loft from the air, and this caused Ned to recall a look he'd seen on her face as he came out of the bar. A quizzical, pondering look she'd directed at him without realizing he'd noticed.

172

So now he sits and thinks. I bet when Jenna told him she'd spotted that flipping loft from the air, he mentioned seeing me there and she's put two and two together. I bet she's sitting in that Micra at this moment, planning how she can slip away and go search the place, so I'd better think of a way to stop her without admitting the gun's there.

As the Volvo speeds towards Haverham and the Micra tags along behind, events are conspiring to make it less and less likely that Jenna will see many happy returns of her birthday.

Sixty-five

They were all having lunch at the Finchs', including Matty. Jenna, impatient to do what had to be done, fretted secretly while playing the birthday girl. It was one fifteen, no food was in evidence, and nobody had started preparing any. A couple of times she caught Ned watching her. *Can't know I've guessed about the loft though, how could he?*

The lunch mystery was solved at half-one when there was a knock at the door. Her parents had ordered a selection of pizzas with all the trimmings, and here they were. Pizza was Jenna's all-time favourite food. She'd to act surprised and delighted as the spread was carried in, though tension over her coming visit to the derelict allotment had knotted her stomach beyond the possibility of appetite.

She did her best with the heaped plateful her mother set in front of her, but after forcing less than half of it into herself she pushed it away. 'Sorry, Mum, but I'm just not hungry, I don't know why.'

Grandad came to her rescue. 'You'd a bit of indigestion after the flight, didn't you, sweetheart? Overexcitement, I reckon.'

'Yes, well.' Amy Finch smiled at her daughter. 'It's

understandable in the circumstances. Why don't you go to your room, darling, lie down quietly for a while. Matty'll be happy enough with us, won't you, Matty?'

Matty nodded. ''Course, Mrs Finch: pizzas like these, I'd be happy on an iceberg in mid Atlantic.' Everybody laughed.

Bit of luck, couldn't have happened better. Jenna pushed back her chair, stood up and smiled at her guests. 'I've had a super time, honestly: best birthday ever. Thanks, everybody. I'll see you soon.' *I hope.* She left the room to the sound of their good wishes.

Now . . . up the stairs, not too quietly. That's it. Now open the bedroom door, shut it firmly, like this. Tiptoe back to the top of the stairs, listen. They're talking, eating. So.

She crept downstairs, lifted her jacket off the newel post and tiptoed to the front door, holding her breath. If somebody came out of the kitchen now she'd have a hard job explaining the jacket over her arm. Nobody did. The latch clicked loudly when she opened the door but Grandad, who hadn't laughed for months, chose this moment to do so. Jenna smiled briefly. *You're doing a great job, aeroplane stone.* She closed the door carefully and hurried away, putting on her jacket as she walked.

Sixty-Six

Munching his fourth slice of hot and hearty with extra pepperoni, Ned thinks, good – with her lying down upstairs I can enjoy my grub without having to watch her every second. *Five minutes later, a spoonful of luxury chocolate mousse with whipped cream and crushed nuts stops half-way to his mouth as a horrible thought strikes him.* How d'you know she's lying down? What if . . .?

He lowers the spoon, pushes back his chair. 'I . . . excuse me a minute.' *He gets up, leaves the kitchen. Jenna's jacket isn't on the newel post.* I knew it. *He takes the steps two at a time, flings open his sister's door. The room is empty.* Oh God, Jen, you're doing it: taking the gun. He'll murder you when he finds out. He'll murder us both.

He must catch her before she reaches the allotments. How long's she been gone? Six, seven minutes. Might do it if I run.

He's started for the door when his mobile chirps. Afterwards he knows he should've ignored it but he isn't thinking straight. He pushes OK on the top step. 'Yeah?'

'Gavin. Slight change of plan for Saturday.'

Change . . .? Surely he can't have guessed? 'Ch . . . change: what sort of change?'

'Not on the phone, dummy. I'm on my way to the loft, I'll see you there in twenty minutes.'

'No!' He reacts too sharply, curses himself inwardly. 'Not there, Gav. I can't make it in the time. How about the park?'

'Sod the park, Finch, I said the loft. You be there, or your relatives'll be scraping you up into three buckets.' He breaks the connection.

Oh Jen. *Ned bounds downstairs and along the hallway. Behind him his mother looks out of the kitchen. 'Ned?' She watches him wrench open the front door, calls after him. 'What's happened, who was that on the phone? Ned!'*

He turns in the doorway. 'Gotta rush, Mum: Jenna. Allotment. Gun.' *The door slams. Amy notices the naked newel post. Both her children gone.*

Sixty-Seven

Gavin Lassiter is halfway across the car park when he spots Ned pelting along West Lane. He shouts, but either Ned doesn't hear or he pretends not to, so Lassiter sets off in pursuit.

I thought so, *he tells himself.* That nosey sister of his is up the allotments, that's why he tried to put me off. No chance though, I could outrun Ned Finch if I'd a leg missing.

He's off the car park and halfway down the slope when he trips. Moving too fast to recover he crashes full-length on the flags, twisting his right knee as he falls. He rolls, cursing, and sits up hugging the injured knee, looking for the tilted flag that tripped him. There's no tilted flag. He notices a crude picture of an aeroplane on one of them, but of course that can't have brought him down. He kneels and pulls himself upright, wincing as the injured knee takes weight. Come on, *he urges, hobbling down on to West Lane*, it's only pain.

Gavin quite likes pain, but he much prefers it to be somebody else's.

Sixty-Eight

There were old men pottering about on some of the allotments. Grandad would have been one of them if it hadn't been for her birthday treat. *Poor Grandad: hope his gun's where I think it is. Hope I get back before anybody misses me. Hope I get back.*

She was scared. Really scared. Gavin Lassiter was no ordinary bully. Bullies duff you up. Smack you, kick your head in. They don't cut your hair off, pull your teeth out. There was something wrong with Gavin, inside his head. It was as if he knew what you were going to do before you did it, like in the park that day. He even had scissors in his pocket.

What if he knows I'm here? She shivered, standing by the rickety gate, gazing at the loft. *Who'll help me if he comes, or if he's here already: these old men?* She shook her head. *Don't be daft, Jen, he's not here, why should he be?* She made herself think about Amy Johnson, alone in the cockpit over shark-infested waters in the middle of a black, black night: the only human being for maybe a thousand miles in any direction. *She* didn't dither, paralysed by her own imaginings. She pressed on. *And so will I.* She pushed the gate, waded in through last year's waist-high weeds.

There was nobody in the loft, but Lassiter had been here. Jenna could feel him, so she didn't want to hang around. Swiftly she scanned the walls, roof braces and floor, trying to think where *she'd* hide a gun. There was no obvious place, but then an obvious place'd be no use, would it?

What about under the floor? She dropped on one knee and started running her fingers along the seams between boards, feeling for a loose one. In stories, things are often concealed under loose floorboards. She found one almost straight away and forced her fingers into the seam till she could prise it up. It came away easily, leaving a narrow black slot a metre long. She laid the board down and thrust her hand into the slot. A few centimetres down her nails dug into cold, damp soil. A smell like mushrooms came off it. She felt about till her knuckles struck something hard, but it was only a lump of mouldering brick. She dropped it and tried again, going down on her stomach to reach as far as she could under the other boards, and it was while she was doing this that she chanced to glance up. She was looking at the underside of the ledge on which, unbeknown to her, Lassiter and her brother had sat on a number of occasions, smoking. The light was poor, but there was enough to reveal a sort of lump clamped like a limpet to the rough plank.

Jenna rose to her knees and hobbled to where she could reach the lump. As soon as she touched it she knew she'd found what she'd come to find. It was smooth and cold, and somebody had secured it to the underside of the ledge with strip after strip of electrician's tape. Working quickly and with her heart pounding, she began ripping away the tape. *He'll know now*, shrilled a voice inside her skull. *You better hurry, hurry, hurry . . .*

What's that? She'd stripped off the last piece of tape and had the gun, surprisingly heavy in her hand, when there

180

came a sound from outside. Still on her knees, she turned to face the door. Somebody was breathing hard, wading through the weeds. *Lassiter*. She lifted the revolver, both hands clasped round the stock like a TV cop. Its darkly gleaming barrel wavered in spite of her grip. She gritted her teeth. *The second I see him I'm gonna . . .*

'Jen?'

Ned. It's Ned. She called out, 'Are you by yourself?'

'Yes. You've found it, haven't you?' He was in the doorway, peering.

'Yes.' She lowered the weapon, breathing out. 'I thought you were . . . I nearly shot you, you idiot.'

'You're the idiot, Jen.' He came forward, hand outstretched. 'Come on, give it to me, we can't do this to Gav. He'll kill us.'

'What?' Jenna scrambled to her feet, held the gun behind her. 'I'm taking it back to Grandad. Nothing can stop me, Ned. If anybody tries, I'll shoot them.'

'Don't be stupid, he's coming, he'll be here any second. Give me the gun and go, before it's too late.'

She shook her head. 'I don't believe you, and anyway he's not having it. Look what he's done to you. I'd rather die than give it to him.'

'Then you probably will, young Finch.'

Brother and sister whirled. Lassiter, hands in pockets, lounged smiling against the doorframe.

Jenna pointed the gun at him. 'Stay back. I'll shoot if you make me.'

Lassiter shook his head. 'I don't think so. I doubt you know how, for a start.'

'Yes I do, everybody does. All I have to do is pull the trigger.'

The boy laughed. 'Go on then.'

'Only if you make me.'

'Oh, I'll make you all right, unless you hand it over. Take it from her, Finch.'

'No!' She swung the barrel towards her brother. 'Nobody takes it.'

Lassiter laughed again. 'You're not going to shoot your own brother, are you?'

'I will if I have to.'

He looked at Ned. 'Sweet little sister you've got, Finch. Control her, *now*, or I will.'

'Listen, Gav.' Ned gazed at the other boy. 'It's no good, is it? Not now. I mean, Jenna's not the only one who knows about . . . you know. You'd be caught straight away, so would I. I'd stick with you if I thought we'd a chance, but . . .'

'Shut up, Finch for God's sake, you make me want to puke.' He looked at Jenna. 'I'm going to walk towards you. You can shoot when you're ready.' He strolled across the floor, limping slightly, taking his time.

Jenna pointed the revolver at his face. 'I'll *do* it, you know.' Her voice was as unsteady as the gun. When two metres separated them she closed her eyes and squeezed the trigger. It wouldn't move.

He darted forward, grabbed the barrel and wrenched the weapon out of her hand. 'I told you you didn't know how. Look.' He held up the gun, thumbed off the safety. 'There's always a catch.' He beckoned with the barrel. 'Get over here with your sister, Finch.' He chuckled. 'You can both blub if you like. It'll cut no ice with me and you know what they say: the family that cries together, dies together.'

It wasn't bad, but he was the only one who laughed.

Sixty-Nine

The Volvo pulls over and halts at the kerb. Matty is first out. 'Wait there, Matty,' raps Peter Finch as he unbelts. Behind him Albert Larwood swings his legs out, stands up. Across the Volvo's roof, the old man sees Matty push open the heavy gate to the allotments and run on to the dirt path between plots. 'Matty!' He starts round the car's rear as his daughter gets out of the front passenger seat. All three adults run to the open gate. The girl's fair head can be seen, bobbing, as she scoots along the path towards Rudyard's derelict patch.

Jen, cries a voice in Matty's head, hold on, I'm coming. She glances back. Jenna's dad is twenty metres away and closing fast, the others well behind. She jinks through the gateway on to a trampled swathe through the weeds. The loft door is open. 'Jen!' she cries as she pelts towards it, and a voice she fears barks from within, 'Stay back, Brewster, or your friend gets it.'

She might have halted if she hadn't been going so fast. As it is, her impetus and anxiety over Jenna carry her to the threshold. As her sudden shadow darkens the interior, Lassiter makes a half-turn towards the door. His right foot comes down on the board Jenna has removed and skates off it into the slot, jarring the injured knee so painfully that he cries out. Before he can recover, Ned darts forward and swings a kick at his groin. The clumpy shoe misses its mark, but the glancing blow it delivers to the ruined kneecap has Lassiter clutching with both hands at the wounded part. Distracted by pain, he hardly notices when the gun falls with a thump on the boards. Matty swoops, scoops up the weapon as Peter Finch arrives at the doorway.

The speed of events has Jenna's head reeling. She slumps down on the ledge, gawping at the new arrivals who are joined a second later by two more. How the heck'd they all get here? She's too much in shock to realize her life has hung by a thread, but when she tries to stand up her legs turn to rubber and she falls on the floor.

Lassiter isn't in shock. His brain, twisted though it may be, is working just fine. His knee, twisted though it certainly is, waits only the brain's command before making one last heroic effort. Momentarily the doorway is congested, but as Jenna hits the floor there's a general surge towards her and he glimpses daylight. Before anyone realizes what's happening he's through the door and away, moving jerkily along the fenceline.

'Leave him, Dad,' growls Peter Finch, helping Jenna to her feet. Albert Larwood, halfway out the door, halts. 'The police'll pick him up. Let's get these kids home, eh?'

Ned and Matty tag along as the parents support Jenna out into the light. Weight reminds Matty she's dangling the gun. 'Here.' She offers it to Ned.

'Huh? Oh, yeah.' He takes it and turns, waiting for his grandad. The old man is pulling the loft door shut. He turns, sees the revolver in Ned's hand. 'Finished with that have you, lad?'

An aching lump fills Ned's throat. He nods. 'Yes, Grandad, I have.' His eyes blur with tears as he returns it to its owner.

Seventy

Lassiter, wounded and dangerous, limps home. His parents are out but he doesn't have long and he knows it. Twenty minutes, tops. That's how long it'll take the Finches to set the law on him.

Starting upstairs he works methodically, wasting no time. In his own room he packs a holdall with clothes, mostly warm stuff and waterproofs. Leaving the holdall at the top of the stairs he goes into his parents' room and rifles the drawers, stuffing his pockets with cash and the best of his mother's jewellery.

He carries the holdall downstairs and puts it by the side door, grabs a plastic carrier in the kitchen and limps through to the front room. It has taken his mother more than twenty years to acquire the seventeen antique snuff-boxes arranged on the sideboard. Today she's gone to an antiques fair with Mr Lassiter, hoping to buy snuffbox number eighteen. Gavin crooks an arm round the collection and sweeps it into the carrier. Start again at one, Mum – give you something to do.

There's nothing else of value in the house. Nothing portable anyway. He crosses to the window, looks up and down the road. All quiet. One more little job and I'm out of here.

He grabs the phone book, looks up Finch. Six entries, only one with a West Lane address. Should be home by now. *He punches in the number. It starts ringing.* Come on. *Seven rings, then a click and a fuzzy message.* Must've run straight to the coppers. *You've reached Amy and Peter's phone. Leave your name and number after the tone and we'll get back to you.* Oh, sure. *He speaks slowly, enunciating every syllable:*

'Sorry I couldn't stay for the rest of your birthday, Jenna, *especially since it's your last. Still, never mind eh? You know we'll see each other again, just once and not for long. What you* don't *know is where and when, but then life'd be a bit dull without surprises, wouldn't it?'*

He breaks the connection, gathers his stuff and leaves the back way, carefully stamping on every one of his father's neatly pricked-out bedding plants as he goes.

Seventy-One

At the Finchs' home on West Lane, Jenna's birthday ends in tears, fears and revelations. First there's Lassiter's message: *especially since it's your last.* Grandad scoffs: calls it the empty gesture of a thwarted nonentity. Ned knows better and so, the day after tomorrow, will Grandad.

Message wiped, Amy and Peter listen unhappily to Ned's confession. 'He had me under like a spell,' he says, speaking of Lassiter. 'He was planning what he called a big job, told me I could be his partner. I knew it wasn't right, but at the same time I felt . . . honoured. When I mentioned the gun – Jenna seeing the gun at your place, Grandad – straight away he had to have it: said he *knew* there was a reason he'd picked me to be his partner. He told me to get the gun so I did. I can't explain. All I can say is I'd have done *anything* for him, till he started bothering Jenna.'

Ned breaks down in tears, and his mother comforts him as her father tells again how he came by the weapon half a century ago in Palestine. '*I* pinched it,' he says, 'so I'd look well condemning somebody for pinching it off me, wouldn't I?'

Peter brews a big pot of tea. Everybody's ready for a cup.

Matty drinks hers, then says she'd better be getting home; it's nearly dark.

'You can't go by yourself,' croaks Jenna. Lassiter's message has been on continuous playback in her skull.

'I'll walk you,' offers Ned, his eyes pink from crying. Matty protests but the boy insists. 'I wouldn't be here if it weren't for you,' he says.

When he returns, Grandad has reached a decision. 'You and I have something to do lad, and we'd best get it over.' They will take the gun to the police station in Keeley. There, Albert Larwood will confess to having hung on to the thing through numerous amnesties, in spite of his late wife's protestations. Ned will tell how he stole the revolver from his grandad's house, and why. 'I suppose we should've done it an hour ago,' says Albert. 'That daft lad'll be miles away by now.'

To their surprise, the officer at the front desk knows quite a lot about Lassiter already. This is because the boy's father has been in, though the officer doesn't tell them this. He confiscates the gun, shaking five snub-nose bullets out of it onto the desktop and scooping them into a plastic bag, growling that he supposes every skunk and his uncle has left fingerprints on it. They're at the station over an hour making statements, having them read back, signing them. 'You'll be hearing from us,' says a weary-voiced sergeant. They believe him.

It's nine o'clock when Grandad drops Ned off and drives away. The last shreds of birthday atmosphere have dissolved, and it is a subdued family that creeps off to bed at half past ten. Jenna lies staring at the ceiling, trying to recapture the thrill of her flight, but it feels like something that happened a long time ago and besides, she can't stop thinking about Lassiter, out there somewhere in the dark. For the first time in years she leaves the light on.

188

Seventy-Two

In the first few weeks of her fifteenth year, Jenna learned something of what it is to feel hunted. Lassiter's message had frightened her, but its impact was magnified a hundredfold when his father's revelations about the boy's past got into the press.

The story broke two days after Lassiter senior's visit to the police station. Nobody seemed to know how it got out but the police were furious, claiming that sensational reportage of this sort was bound to affect the chance of a fair trial once the youth was apprehended.

Jenna's parents tried to keep the story from her but failed. They couldn't keep her off school, and talk in the yard was of nothing else. It seemed that at eleven, Gavin Lassiter had set fire to his school in the Midlands after being given a detention. Nobody was hurt, but the school was totally destroyed and a number of hamsters, gerbils and goldfish perished. The Lassiters left the area a few weeks after the incident to shield Gavin from possible questioning.

Just over a year later two boys, brothers who'd befriended him at his new school, came to suspect that Gavin had been responsible for a holdup at a filling station and told the police. Gavin was questioned but his parents gave him an alibi and he was never charged. Not long afterwards Lassiter, masked and wielding a *panga*, ambushed the brothers separately and hacked off their thumbs. He was suspected of course, but again his parents lied for him and he was released.

There were other stories, equally gruesome and for Jenna, terrifying. Police all over the country were looking for Lassiter, and Matty told her friend it was hardly likely he'd risk coming back to Haverham just to avenge himself on her, but Jenna wasn't convinced. It seemed to her the boy must have supernatural powers to have got away with his crimes: powers he'd use to evade capture even in Haverham as he came to take her ears, her teeth, her eyes. She started having nightmares. It got so bad she didn't dare walk to and from school so her grandad drove her, dropping her at the gate in the morning and outside the house in the afternoon. He drove Matty too, though she claimed not to be worried.

Flight, that brief bright realm of soaring promise, sank and shrank till it didn't seem real any more.

Then, during the course of a single gorgeous week in June, everything was mended. On the Monday afternoon, Gavin Lassiter was arrested at Stranraer while boarding a ferry for Ireland. The Keeley police phoned Amy Finch who burst into tears, thanked God and called Jenna at school. Her grandad picked her and Matty up just the same, but for once it was a transport of delight.

Two days later, Ned and his grandad received identical letters from the police. Taking account of all the circumstances, the Chief Constable had decided not to proceed against either of them on this occasion in the matter of offences committed. However, it was hoped that recent events had given them pause, and that they would have no truck in future with firearms, burglary or the planning of robberies.

And then came Saturday, and the best thing of all. Lunch was planned as a re-run of Jenna's birthday meal with Grandad coming, and Matty, and the delivery boy with armfuls of pizzas and all the trimmings. The only missing ingredients would be fear and lurking guilt, and nobody was going to miss them.

They ate in the garden. The sun shone, the birds sang, the food was delicious and everybody was happy, but that wasn't it. No. The best thing was when Grandad stood up at his end of the picnic table and announced he'd got something to say. Everybody stopped chattering and looked at him. 'Speech!' cried Ned, and the others smiled and nodded.

Grandad shook his head. ''Tisn't exactly a speech, Ned: more like an announcement.' He cleared his throat. 'Four months, two weeks and one day ago I lost Grandma, the best pal a man ever had.' The listeners lowered their eyes, nodded and murmured. 'Oh yes,' he continued, 'it's sad, right enough. Sad she can't be here: she loved a picnic, my Alice.' He shook his head. 'For a while I thought I'd die, or lose my mind. I'd lost all interest in the world. Then, one day, this young lady,' nodding at Jenna, 'came to my sad little house and told me she wanted to fly, and suddenly I felt like old Rudyard must've felt every time he freed those blessed pigeons of his and watched 'em soar. You see,' he smiled ruefully, '*I* wanted to fly, right from being a little lad. It was Amy Johnson put that in my head, only it wasn't any use 'cause I'd no father and we'd no money. My mother told me I'd never fly and she was right in a way: I'll never be a pilot but you see, there are ways you can fly without your feet ever leaving the ground. Flying kites is one way, and some

191

old men fly pigeons. I haven't got a kite or a pigeon but I've got something a hundred times better, namely a granddaughter with a natural aptitude for flying, and the long and short of it is, Grandma had some life insurance and I've talked to her and she agrees with me that it'd be a good use of the money if it got our Jenna some lessons.'

And that's it; the best thing of all. Jenna got her lessons and went on to college and now she's an airline captain. Ned chose his friends more carefully after Gavin Lassiter and grew up to get cash with a card, not a revolver. Matty read anthropology at university and is somewhere in Africa, helping chimpanzees. Amy and Peter still live in Haverham. Thomas the cat crossed West Lane once too often and got halfway.

Grandad Larwood? He learned to get along without his best pal for a time but he's with her now, under the sycamores in the churchyard a few metres from the flagstone he carved as a boy and he's in the sky too, gentle on his granddaughter's mind as she steers her silver bird among the clouds.